THE STONE SPEAKS

"Torin?" Breddo grabbed Kellach's shoulders with a death grip. "Torin, Torin, you've got to help me."

"But, I'm not—" Kellach began to explain, but Breddo wouldn't listen.

"Listen to me. I've seen too much. I know I shouldn't have eavesdropped. I shouldn't have tried to see. But the scream, her scream . . . I thought I could help, could tell you about it, but I'm forgetting. My mind . . . it feels like sewer mush. I heard too much. I can't fight it anymore. You have to stop them. The stone . . . speaks. It will show you the way. The cell at the end of the corridor—the end of the corridor—you have to see . . ."

Breddo's eyes fluttered, and he fell to the ground.

Book 1
Secret of the Spiritkeeper
Matt Forbeck

Book 2
Riddle in Stone
Ree Soesbee

Book 3
Sign of the Shapeshifter
Dale Donovan and Linda Johns
(October 2004)

Book 4
Eye of Fortune
Denise R. Graham
(December 2004)

RIDDLE in STONE

REE SOESBEE

KNIGHTS
OF THE
SILVER
DRAGON

BOOK 2

COVER & INTERIOR ART
EMILY FIEGENSHUH

MIRROR
STONE

Riddle in Stone

©2004 Wizards of the Coast, Inc.

Distributed in the United States by Holtzbrinck Publishing. Distributed in Canada by Fenn Ltd.

Distributed to the hobby, toy, and comic trade in the United States and Canada by regional distributors.

Distributed worldwide by Wizards of the Coast, Inc. and regional distributors.

Cover art by Emily Fiegenschuh
First Printing: August 2004
Library of Congress Catalog Card Number: 2004101144

9 8 7 6 5 4 3 2 1

US ISBN: 0-7869-3211-2
UK ISBN: 0-7869-3212-0
620-96531-001-EN

U.S., CANADA,
ASIA, PACIFIC, & LATIN AMERICA
Wizards of the Coast, Inc.
P.O. Box 707
Renton, WA 98057-0707
+1-800-324-6496

EUROPEAN HEADQUARTERS
Wizards of the Coast, Belgium
T Hofveld 6d
1702 Groot-Bijgaarden
Belgium
+322 457 3350

Visit our website at **www.mirrorstonebooks.com**

This book is gratefully dedicated to Princess D,
who gave me her friendship and her beanbag—
upon which most of this novel was written.
What more could a person ask for?

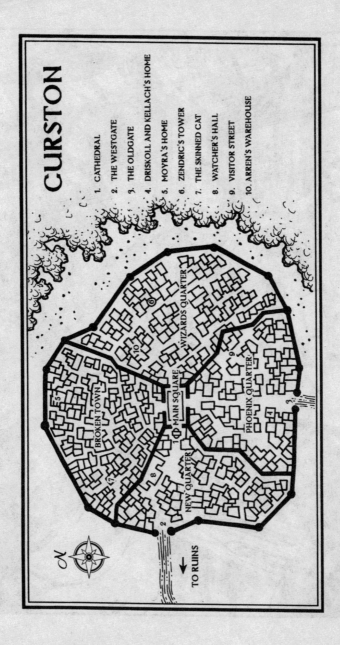

CURSTON

1. CATHEDRAL
2. THE WESTGATE
3. THE OLDGATE
4. DRISKOLL AND KELLACH'S HOME
5. MOYRA'S HOME
6. ZENDRIC'S TOWER
7. THE SKINNED CAT
8. WATCHER'S HALL
9. VISITOR STREET
10. ARREN'S WAREHOUSE

BROKEN TOWN

WIZARDS QUARTER

MAIN SQUARE

NEW QUARTER

PHOENIX QUARTER

TO RUINS

CHAPTER

1

"Honey drop, boy?" A hawker pressed a piece of golden candy into Kellach's hand. "Only half a coin!"

All along the street where Kellach stood, colorful streamers swung in the wind. Silver dragon banners hung from balconies. Shopkeepers stood outside their stores, handing out samples and festival tokens to every passerby.

Kellach dug deep into his stained apprentice robes and pulled out enough change for two. He passed a candy to his younger brother, Driskoll.

"Let's go, Kellach," Driskoll said, biting off the top of the sugary stick. "Dad's waiting for us in Main Square."

Kellach stared at a carriage breezing past, drawn by white horses. The girl in the carriage waved. Kellach smiled dumbly.

Driskoll tugged on Kellach's sleeve.

"Come on, Kell, stop gawking at the tourists. If we're late for the first day of the Promise Festival, Dad might not have time to give me my Promise gift."

"Okay, okay." Kellach began walking briskly down the street.

He looked back over his shoulder at Driskoll. "Well, hurry up!"

Driskoll sighed and jogged to catch up with his brother. "Do you think I'll get a new sword?"

Kellach rolled his eyes. "You've been hinting at it to Dad for the last six weeks. If he hasn't figured it out, he's as dense as rock."

"What do you think Zendric will get you for Promise Day?" Driskoll wondered aloud. "All the apprentices get gifts on the first day of the Promise Festival. I heard the jeweler's apprentice got a golden toolbox. And in the cathedral, all the acolytes got new robes. Zendric's sure to give you something really cool!"

"Last year, he gave me a book."

"Another one?"

"Shut up. It was a new spell." Kellach muttered, "Maybe this year, he'll get me a familiar. All the other apprentice wizards have one. Sarad got a kitten. He says he's going to train it to turn the pages of his books for him while he casts. And Delwin got a hawk."

"I'd rather have a sword, like Dad's," Driskoll said. "He's taught me more this year than ever before—all about feints and parries and overhand blows!" Driskoll grinned. "Wow, with a real sword, I could make up my own stories and then sing about them at the festival. I'd be a hero. I'd . . . I'd . . . "

" . . . put out your own eye," Kellach broke in. "Come on, Driskoll. You hardly know how to use a sword. You'd run at your own shadow."

Kellach did a strange little dance down the street, miming a swordsman fumbling through an attack and dropping his sword.

"Good luck getting a sword. Dad would be smarter to get

you a shield. No sharp edges for you to hurt yourself." His sunny smile took most of the sting from the words. "Come on, let's go. We'll be lucky if we don't miss the opening ceremony."

"I don't need luck," Driskoll said grumpily, following his brother down the road toward Main Square. "I just need a sword."

∎ ∎ ∎ ∎ ∎

At the edge of the square, a performer juggled flaming clubs. A thick crowd of onlookers surrounded him. Driskoll and Kellach ducked beneath elbows and squeezed past a plump woman carrying a crying baby.

"Watch it, boys!" the woman called.

Smiling and waving to her, Driskoll and Kellach dodged another merchant—this one selling candied turnips. They pushed through the crowd toward the center of the square.

Flags hung on long poles all around the square's stone courtyard. A low stage, covered with a canopy, stood in front of the obelisk marking the middle of the square. To the right of the platform sat a large bundle wrapped in a red silk sheet. From the top of the stage canopy hung tapestries of dragon battles and victorious knights.

The Promise Festival was a reminder of the glory days of Curston, before the seal was sundered and monsters wreaked havoc on the town. Long ago, the town was known as Promise. It was a place of peace and prosperity. Now, for three days every year, it remembered the past.

"Cinnamon buns! Cinnamon buns!" a baker yelled. A group of guards from the city watch snatched the buns off her tray. The sweet scent of vanilla and cinnamon drifted through the air.

"That smells delicious!" Driskoll said as he headed for the stand.

Kellach tugged at his collar and pulled him away. "Those are for the watchers."

"Kellach! Driskoll!" a familiar voice called.

Looking over the heads of those around them, Kellach spotted their father standing among a group of watchers.

"Dad!" he called, waving back.

The boys pushed through the crowd to meet him. Tall and burly, Torin stood proudly in his fine captain's garb. The symbol of the city of Curston shone in gold thread upon his chest.

"Staying out of trouble, boys?" Torin asked, his voice rough and commanding. He took a large bite from a cinnamon bun.

Kellach rolled his eyes. "Yes, Dad. We're going by Zendric's tower later so he can give me my Promise gift."

"Well, that's the Promise Festival tradition, I suppose." Torin nodded. "A gift to help you along the road of a journeyman in your craft."

Driskoll could hardly contain his anticipation, hopping lightly from foot to foot.

"Well, Driskoll," Torin continued. "As you aren't formally apprenticed to anyone, that means I'm your master this Promise Day."

Torin's stern gaze made Driskoll stand still.

"Now, I have to tell you, Kellach," Torin said. "After all you boys have put me through lately, I wasn't sure if I should give your brother a gift. And I have to admit that I had no idea what he'd like."

Kellach covered a snort of laughter.

4

"But I think I found something." Torin drew a long belt from behind his back and held it out to Driskoll. The belt was tooled of thick leather. It had faint emblems of eagles on the length and was dyed an even, rich black.

Driskoll's face fell.

"A belt?" he said. He took it gently, staring down at it. With a weak smile, he gazed up at his father. *"Uh* . . . Thank you, Dad. Thanks. Really."

Torin continued, his expression never changing, "I thought you could use it . . . ," he reached out toward one of his watchers, "to hang this on."

The watcher handed him a long black scabbard and a shining sword. The sword handle was red and the pommel tipped with gold. Engraved down the blade was a single falcon, spiraling in flight. Torin slipped the blade into the scabbard, and Driskoll grabbed the sword with a wide smile.

"Happy Promise Day, Driskoll," Torin said gruffly. "Next week, I'll teach you some new disarms with that. But until then, be careful with it."

"I will, Dad." Driskoll glowed as he buckled his new belt and attached the sword. "Thank you."

"Now off you go, boys. The opening ceremony is about to begin." Torin stalked off with the other watchers, and the two boys headed for the stage.

As they stood in the back of the audience, Driskoll fingered his new sword. "Check this out, Kellach! It's got a falcon on the blade! See? It really looks like it's taking flight!"

Kellach smiled then playfully punched Driskoll in the shoulder. "Look, it's started. There's Pralthamus."

5

"Who?" Driskoll looked up.

Kellach pointed at the center of the platform. "The new magistrate."

A portly man rose from his seat and stepped to the front of the stage, shuffling his notes self-consciously. His face looked pale, with the exception of reddened cheeks. His hair had long ago turned from black to a peppery gray. He smiled broadly, as if hoping that the crowd could not see his nervousness through his even, white teeth.

Along the back of the platform sat the members of Curston's ruling council— two men and a woman. The expressions on their faces ranged from amused to stern.

"Where's Zendric?" Driskoll whispered. "Isn't he supposed to be up there with the rest of the ruling council?" He hopped up and down on one foot to see over the heads of the crowd.

"*Ssshh* . . . He's probably late," Kellach replied. "Got stuck in the crowd or something."

"Citizens of Curston," Pralthamus boomed. A broad smile spread across the magistrate's face as the crowd murmured his name. "This year's Promise Festival brings a new era of statue . . ."

The crowd laughed.

Pralthamus cleared his throat. "No. Wait." The magistrate flipped through his notes. "I mean, prosperity! A new era of prosperity."

The audience applauded. Pralthamus grinned again and ran his fingers through his salt-and-pepper hair.

He continued, "Adventurers from all across the kingdoms are coming here to destroy the beasts of the ruins. We've opened our

6

gates to these travelers, but we must be wary of the implistations . . . *uh* . . . implications." He grimaced and fluttered through the notes once more. "Several watchers, our friends and family, have vanished within the last few weeks. This only points a finger toward the dangers that surround our town . . ."

"Watchers disappearing?" Driskoll's brow furrowed. "That's bad."

"Yeah." Kellach peered around at the watchers patrolling the plaza. "I heard Dad talking about it the other night. About two weeks ago, one of the watchers at the prison was reported missing. Then, a young recruit vanished while on patrol. There's been no trace of either one."

"What's that thing?" Driskoll stood on his tiptoes, trying to see over the crowd.

Pralthamus gestured toward a silk-wrapped bundle standing to the side of the platform. "And now may I present a gift to the city from one of its more prestigious members. The artist was kind enough to model the face of this lovely statue in the image of Elisa Greyson. Although she went missing two weeks ago, we still hold hope that she will return to us in safety. This statue is dedicated to all those watchers who have given their service to our city. They protect us from darkness, and we remember their names."

Pralthamus tugged on the cord that kept the bundle wrapped.

Nothing happened.

Flustered, Pralthamus tugged again, this time with both hands. But the knots stayed firm. He laughed awkwardly, making a grand sweep with his other arm as though to encompass the statue.

Pralthamus tugged again. The sheet shivered but did not fall.

"They protect us from darkness, and we remember their names!" The magistrate jerked on the cord with all his might. This time the cord flew off, hurling the sheet over Pralthamus and the other people on the stage.

Driskoll and Kellach roared with laughter. The crowd around them applauded and whistled as the magistrate and the council fought with the large red sheet.

Finally, they threw off the cover. Pralthamus's dark gray hair was rumpled and his eyes blinked in the bright sunlight. He sidestepped the still-fluttering sheet and held up his hands. The crowd quieted.

"Well, I . . . , " he mumbled, a faint smile touching his lips. "I . . . oh never mind. Just be careful and enjoy the Promise Festival, everyone!" Pralthamus stepped off the platform, scattering his notes as he hit the ground.

"Come on," Kellach said. "Let's get a better look at that statue." He tugged Driskoll's arm, leading him through the crowd to the side of the platform.

The statue was life-size, carved from a single piece of elegant marble. The woman's hair was covered by a graceful hood, and she held a lowered sword in her right hand. The long sleeves of the robe lay in delicate folds, covering strong arms that seemed almost to be ready to move at any moment. Although her face was partially covered by the stone hood, she had a strange look upon her shadowed features, as if she had just unraveled some great mystery.

"Her face looks familiar," Driskoll frowned.

"Don't you remember her?" Kellach said. "Elisa was one of the watchers assigned to guard the prison."

Kellach crouched down. Strange circular symbols covered the base of the statue. The same characters were repeated along its robe. "Interesting," he murmured. "This doesn't look like any language I've ever seen."

"Probably just some artist thing." Driskoll scanned the statue. A stumpy third arm seemed to poke out from beneath the figure's left sleeve. "You know, this artist may have gotten the face right, but the body is bizarre! There are three arms!"

Driskoll moved closer to the statue to poke the strange stone arm. But before he could make contact, the arm reached out and grabbed his shoulder.

Driskoll screamed.

CHAPTER

2

"Sssshhh! It's just me!" Moyra pulled Driskoll behind the statue. She was dressed from head to toe in blue-gray clothes, chosen to match the stone of most of Curston's buildings. She blended in so well with the statue Driskoll hadn't realized she was there at all.

Moyra pulled a gray cap off her head, revealing a bright shock of red hair. "I've been looking all over for you, boys."

Kellach rose to his feet and smiled. "Hi, Moyra! I was wondering when you were planning to say hello."

"What are you doing back here?" Driskoll asked.

"Keeping a low profile." Moyra's eyes darted through the crowd. "The baker accused me of stealing some cinnamon buns. But I didn't do it."

Driskoll crossed his arms. "Yeah, sure."

"Never mind," Moyra said. "Listen, are you two busy? Tell me you're not busy. I need your help." Her green eyes were pleading. "It's my dad."

"Breddo?" Driskoll asked. "What's he done now?"

Moyra's father, Breddo, was a notorious pickpocket, a good-natured thief who enjoyed the finer things. But he found himself, more often than not, paying for them in Curston's prison.

Moyra punched Driskoll in the arm. "He hasn't done anything! He's being released today. I was hoping the two of you would go to the prison with me."

"Why can't you go by yourself?" Kellach asked.

Moyra looked away. "I promised my mom I wouldn't go alone. She heard about the watcher who disappeared." Moyra thumbed back at the statue of Elisa. "She's afraid it's dangerous or something. She'd go with me, but she has to stay here and sell her weaving. If we're lucky, she'll sell enough this week to feed us for three months. She can't possibly get away right now.

"Besides the guards at Watchers' Hall love you boys. I figured with you along . . ." Moyra's voice trailed off, and her green eyes glanced up at Kellach.

Kellach sighed.

Driskoll stepped forward and bowed. "I'd be glad to be of service, milady. With my new sword, I will protect you from any danger!"

Moyra bowed in reply.

"Don't encourage him, Moyra," Kellach grumped.

"That means you're coming, right?" She looked at Kellach and flashed her charming smile.

Kellach looked down quickly and brushed off his robes. "Of course," he muttered.

"Shouldn't we tell Dad we're leaving?" Driskoll glanced at Kellach.

"We already told him we were going to Zendric's to get my

Promise gift," Kellach said. "We can go to the prison and then swing by Zendric's tower on the way home."

Kellach looked over at their father, standing proudly in front of the stage next to Pralthamus. "He probably won't even notice that we're gone."

∎ ∎ ▮ ∎ ∎

Curston's prison sat under Watchers' Hall, a few blocks from Main Square. Although Watchers' Hall wasn't a long walk from the plaza, it took the kids a long time to get there. Vendors lined the road, their carts full of cheap swords and steel trinkets. Groups of people bunched in front of each cart, watching and cheering as the hawkers haggled with their customers.

"You'd think these people have nothing better to do than go shopping." Kellach dodged a pair of elves testing out a sword. "Hey, watch where you're pointing that thing!"

"It's just after lunchtime," Driskoll mourned. "I bet the merchants in Main Square are starting to give away the extras now: sausage rolls, chocolate pastries, berry pies . . ."

"Don't worry, Driskoll, the Promise Festival lasts three whole days." Moyra smiled. "That's plenty of time to sample the festival food. We should be back in Main Square in less than an hour. Maybe my dad will take us to see the fire jugglers, like last year!"

The wide gates of Watchers' Hall hung open. Their oak boards were weathered with age and rain. Everburning torches sat in burnished sconces, lighting the shadowy entryway. Two watchers flanked the doorway, leaning heavily on their swords. Neither one of them greeted the kids as they walked past.

Kellach gripped Driskoll's hand. "Driskoll," he whispered,

glancing at the guards, "do these watchers look—I don't know— *normal* to you?"

"Yeah, of course," Driskoll replied cheerily. "That's Sedrick and Tonna. We see them all the time."

"But do they *look* normal? Have you ever seen Sedrick like that before?" Kellach indicated the tall, thin watcher at the right side of the entrance. He did not move, staring down at his sword as though in deep thought. He had a strange, pleasant smile on his face.

"Well, it is the Promise Festival," Driskoll said. "Maybe he's just taking it easy today." He shrugged.

"It's not like Sedrick to ever stand still."

"I'm sure it's nothing, Kellach," Driskoll said.

Moyra broke into a run. "Come on!" They rushed past the tower stairs and into the adjacent prison office.

The watcher sitting behind the office desk looked up as they approached. He grinned broadly as he recognized the boys. Guffy had lost a leg to a werewolf in the weeks after the Sundering. The kind old man had been stationed at a desk for years.

Guffy grabbed his crutch and stood up, his lanky body covered by a slightly too-short tunic bearing the symbol of the city of Curston. He stumped forward to greet them.

"Kellach, Driskoll!" After a moment, he squinted at their red-haired companion. "Moyra, is it?"

"Yes, sir," Moyra said, an uncharacteristic touch of cheer in her voice. She was excited to see her dad and it showed in her smile.

"How've you been, Guffy?" Kellach smiled, clasping the grandfatherly man's outstretched hand.

"Been good. Knee aches a bit, but it doesn't bother me. Zendric was here earlier, took a look at it for me while he had the time," Guffy said. "What can I do for you?"

"We're here for a prisoner release," Moyra said. "My dad."

"Ha!" chuckled Guffy. "Is Breddo on his way out again? All but a permanent visitor here. We'll miss his pennywhistle from the cells at night. Well, I'm sure he'll be back soon."

Moyra scowled.

"You'll have to talk to Sergeant Gult," Guffy said. "He's in charge of releases these days. There have been a lot of changes in the watch system lately. Troublesome at best. But, with watchers going missing, it can't be helped. Let me show you the way."

Guffy turned and led them down a short hallway into a small chamber.

The walls were dark, nearly black. Even the light streaming in the narrow window did little to lighten the room. The ceiling was low, but a cheery fire lit the small fireplace.

A burly watcher sat on a rickety chair in front of the hearth. He held a pipe in one hand and a sticky bun covered in icing in the other.

As Guffy led the three kids inside, the man looked up. He inhaled the cinnamon bun in one bite and glared at the visitors.

"Here, now, who've you brought in, Guffy?" he asked as he licked the icing from his thick fingers.

"The captain's lads and a girl from the town, Gult," Guffy replied. "Her father's due to be released today." Guffy wrinkled his face, making shooing gestures at the heavy man to encourage him to stand.

Gult squinted a bit, taking in Moyra's red hair and slight

build. "Breddo's gal, eh? You look like him." He leaned back in his chair and took another cinnamon bun from the basket on the hearth. He lifted the bun to his lips. "Sorry. I'm busy." Bits of cinnamon bun fell from his mouth as he spoke.

Kellach stepped forward. "I'm sure my father will be interested in hearing about what's keeping you so busy."

Gult cursed and rose from his seat. He glared at Moyra. "You'll have to sign Breddo out. You know how to sign your name, girl?"

Moyra gritted her teeth. "Yes."

"Good." Gult waddled over to a small desk and picked up a pile of papers. He spent a great deal of time flipping through them, settling at last on a thick folder with Breddo's name clearly labeled across the top.

"I'm surprised he found it," Moyra grumbled.

"I'm surprised he can read it." Kellach winked, and Moyra had to smile.

"Breddo, Breddo. Petty larceny, weaponless burglary . . . Says here, we're to keep a cell ready for him. Frequent visitor, he is!" Gult guffawed. "Looks here like he was moved once already. He's in the deep now."

"You go get him, Gult." Guffy tapped his fingers on the desk. "That's a good fellow."

Gult scowled but obeyed Guffy's order. "Wait here." He pulled a thick ring of keys from his pocket and waddled down the hallway.

"If you want a sticky bun while you wait, we've got plenty," Guffy said. The elderly watcher lifted the basket. His face fell. "Or, *er,* we had plenty. I can go find you more. The merchants

15

were very kind this year, sending us all sorts of sweets. Twice as many as last year." Guffy smiled, showing three missing teeth.

"No, really, we've got to get my father and be going." Moyra couldn't help frowning.

"Right." Driskoll murmured sorrowfully, kicking a bit of lint across the floor. "No time for a snack." Kellach shot him an exasperated look, and the younger boy fell silent.

Guffy nodded, setting down the basket, and then stepped toward the door. "If you've need of me, I'll be in my office. I've got to get back to my duties." He winked at Moyra, then left the three alone in the dim room.

Gult seemed to take forever. Out the window, Kellach could see the bright banners of the Promise Festival. Occasionally a bit of music or laughter wafted in from the road.

At last Gult stormed through the door, his face covered in a sheen of sweat. "They moved him again, they did," the fat man grunted, slamming his keys down on the table. "Took me forever to find him."

The boys peered past the big watcher, eager for their first view of Moyra's laughing, robust father. Breddo should have been pushing past the watcher with a clever hello, his arms open for a quick hug from his daughter, and a laugh on his lips. But no one came through the doorway.

Outside, they heard clanking chains and the sounds of shuffling in the darkness.

Moyra rushed to the doorway. Her face went pale. "Daddy?" she whispered. "What have they done to you?"

Breddo moved forward, drawn by the familiar sound of Moyra's voice. He was hunched, and his clothing hung from a thin skeleton. His hair, red and bright like his daughter's, stood up, the color brilliant against his washed-out complexion. Breddo's hands shivered, and the chains around his wrists clanked loudly. He stepped toward his daughter and then shrank back as she reached out for him.

"Moyra?" he whispered, his voice hoarse.

Moyra rounded on the fat watcher. "What happened to him?" she yelled. "What did you do?"

"Do? Nothing," Gult replied. "I think his term just didn't agree with him." He flipped open another sheaf of papers and began filling out a release form, completely ignoring the girl.

"Breddo, are you all right?" Driskoll asked, taking the poor man's arm.

Breddo trembled against his hand but stared down at the boy with a faint recognition. "Torin's boy?" he whispered.

"If he's injured, I swear, I'll . . . I'll . . . " Moyra stormed to the table and hurled the papers into the air. As the parchment drifted to the floor, she shouted, "He's not some animal! How could you treat him like this?"

"Like what?" Gult tromped to Breddo's side, grabbing the man's wrists roughly and unlocking the chains that held his wrists together. "I've done my duty, and you'll not be telling me how to do it. He was fed and watered, same as always. They had to move him because he nearly broke out of his old cell."

Gult picked the release form off the floor and held it out to Moyra. "Are you going to sign this and get on out of here? Or am I going to rip this up and put your father back in the hole?"

Moyra's eyes blazed.

Before she could say anything, Kellach placed his hand

on Moyra's shoulders. "He's okay, Moyra. Let's just get out of here."

"I'm going to report you. You'll see. You won't treat my father like this again!" Moyra quickly signed the form, took Breddo's hand in hers, and stepped backward toward the door.

"You want him treated better?" Gult laughed. "Then keep him out of jail!"

■   ■   ▌   ▌   ▌

Kellach thought he could still hear Gult's mocking laughter as they led Breddo home.

"They didn't beat him, Moyra," Kellach said in a low tone. "He's got no marks of it. He just looks overwrought, like he's been under a lot of stress."

Breddo leaned heavily on Kellach's shoulder. Moyra said nothing, gripping Breddo's hand with white knuckles. They picked their way through the festival crowds on the streets. People were still out celebrating—singing songs and buying gifts—but none of the kids felt any happiness at the sight.

"Whatever happened to him," Kellach said. "I don't think the watchers did it. I've never heard of any kind of abuses within the prison before. In fact, Dad always complains that the guards are sneaking snacks down to the prisoners."

"Or letting them out to play cards," Driskoll chimed in.

"He didn't get that way playing cards," Moyra replied acidly, running a hand through her coppery hair in exasperation.

"Stone . . . stone . . . ," Breddo murmured, squeezing his daughter's hand.

Moyra's house in Broken Town was a small building wedged

in between a bustling inn and a row of gypsy stores that came and went with the seasons. A gang of half-orcs on the corner stared at them as they walked past. Kellach shivered.

Moyra blushed when she saw the look on his face. She pulled the key to their small home from her pocket, the rusted tines more like a small fork than a guardian device. It slipped into the battered oak door atop the rotting porch, and the door swung open.

Despite its outward appearance, the interior of Moyra's home looked comfortable. A long purple sofa covered with a woven blanket sat in the middle of the small room. Shelves filled with brightly colored pottery lined the walls.

Moyra reached to help Breddo into the front room. But Breddo pulled away in panic.

"No, I won't go back in there!" he cried, shuffling backward. Breddo plunged his hands into his hair, tugging violently as he fell to his knees in the street.

"Daddy, we're home." Moyra gripped his hand and tried to pull Breddo to his feet.

The man whimpered, his eyes seeking some escape from a fate only he could see.

"Breddo!" Kellach stepped in, using his larger bulk to help Moyra. "You've got to get up."

For a moment, Moyra's father seemed to focus, fixing his eyes on Kellach's face. "Torin?" Breddo grabbed his shoulders with a death grip. "Torin, Torin, you've got to help me."

"But, I'm not—" Kellach began to explain, but Breddo wouldn't listen.

"Listen to me. I've seen too much. I know I shouldn't have

eavesdropped. I shouldn't have tried to see. But the scream, her scream . . . I thought I could help, could tell you about it, but I'm forgetting. My mind . . . it feels like sewer mush. I heard too much. I can't fight it anymore. You have to stop them. The stone . . . speaks. It will show you the way. The cell at the end of the corridor—the end of the corridor—you have to see . . . "

Breddo's eyes fluttered, and he fell to the ground.

CHAPTER

3

"Daddy?" Moyra shook her father's arms. His eyelids snapped open but his eyes looked vacant. "Help me get him up," she said.

Kellach, Moyra, and Driskoll lifted Breddo, half carrying him into the house. Moyra turned to her friends as they placed her father on the couch. Although Breddo was still murmuring to himself, his words were no longer frantic.

"I think he'll be all right. I'm just going to let him sleep," Moyra said. "Whatever happened to him, it's taken a lot out of him."

She walked her friends to the door.

"Thanks for your help." Her face reddened. "I'm sorry you had to see him like this. But you will tell your dad about this, won't you? Tell him what they did to my father—"

Before she could say anything else, a low cry from Breddo issued from the front room. Moyra looked back over her shoulder. "I'd better go," she said. Then she closed the door.

"That was weird." Driskoll eyed the closed door before turning to Kellach. "I've never seen anyone act like that before."

"He wasn't himself. Something has changed him." Rubbing his chin thoughtfully, Kellach turned and began to walk back through the streets of Broken Town.

Running quickly so he wouldn't be left behind, Driskoll blurted, "What do you mean?"

Kellach considered. "It's like something's affected his mind—altered his brain somehow. Like a drug, or a spell, making him see things that aren't there, and making it difficult for him to remember even the simplest things."

"What do you think happened to him?"

"I'm not sure yet," Kellach admitted grimly. "But I think we should find out. And the best person to help us with that is Zendric. "

Driskoll grinned. "And while we're there, we can get your Promise gift! Let's go!"

Kellach's steps were light and sure, walking a path through the city that he knew well from his studies with Zendric, the wizard who taught Kellach magic. They traveled deep into the Wizard's Quarter on the east side of town, meandering through the twisted streets and past odd shops of wizard's tools. In a private corner near the city wall, Kellach came to a stop outside Zendric's tower.

"A fence?" Driskoll asked. "That's new."

A small but formidable fence now circled the tower. The metal bars coiled into shapes of phoenixes, dragons, and other mythical beasts.

"Zendric put this in about a month ago, after what happened with Lexos," Kellach said.

Driskoll shuddered at the sound of their old enemy's name. Though Lexos was safely behind bars now, he had tried to kill Zendric and almost gotten away with it.

"He said it was for security. But I think he just likes the way it looks." Kellach reached to push the gate open but paused when he noted a horse standing in the yard beyond.

"Zendric's got a visitor," Kellach said, curiously peering through the gate at the animal. It was a dark, common traveling pony with little to mark its origin. With a quick study, he also noted that the horse had no sword hanging from the saddle and no mark where one might have lain. "Whoever it is, it isn't one of the watchers."

"Maybe a trader?" Driskoll murmured, keeping his voice low.

Kellach shook his head. "On one horse? With only light saddlebags?" He pointed to the small packages laced to the saddle. They were barely large enough to contain a change of clothing, a few supplies, and a bedroll.

Driskoll pushed past his brother, kneeling to put his head beneath Kellach's so that he could peer in as well. "Another wizard, I'll bet. A wizard who has come for the Promise Festival or to trade spells with Zendric."

"A wizard would have runes carved on the saddle, for protection," Kellach said. "There would be an aura of magic around it. And a real wizard would have an extra pack on the horse to carry his scrolls and books, his ink and paper. I don't see anything like that, either. But I do see a ladies' saddle, and the stirrups are too small for a man."

"Ooh," Driskoll chuckled. "Maybe Zendric's met a girl."

Kellach reddened. "I seriously doubt that."

"Why not?" He raised an eyebrow.

Kellach snorted, opening the gate. The well-oiled hinges did not make a squeak. "I think we should go look. He didn't show up at the opening ceremony, and now he's got a strange visitor. Zendric might be in trouble." Quietly, he slipped through the gate.

Slowly, Driskoll followed, walking into the small yard of Zendric's tower. Kellach passed the horse, patting it gently so that it would make no sound as he went by, and then pushed aside the bushes beneath Zendric's front windows. As the boys drew closer, a pair of voices from above caught their attention.

" . . . in danger." A woman's voice whispered through the window. Kellach caught a faint glimpse of a purple velvet cloak. Quickly, Kellach grabbed Driskoll's shoulder and they both crouched down beneath the windowsill.

"Wyrmserum is dangerous, my dear." The boys exchanged glances, recognizing the voice. It was Zendric.

"Wyrmserum?" Driskoll mouthed. Kellach poked him with his elbow.

"It will be done," the woman whispered. Driskoll froze, clamping a hand over his mouth. Kellach saw gloved hands clutch the windowsill above him. She must be standing just inside, her back to the wizard. Her voice was cruel. "I will not fail this task!"

"No one will suspect us." For the first time, Zendric sounded harsh. "If you will listen to me and keep your temper and your patience, we will have it. I promise you that."

"Keep my patience?" the woman hissed. The hair rose on Kellach's neck. Her hiss sounded like a snake. "I have done so. I grow weary of the wait. Soon, there will be death, and there will be pain."

Footsteps paced the room above them, and the woman walked away from the window. The boys breathed a collective sigh of relief.

"We are not yet finished," Zendric murmured. "Only a few more days."

The woman's voice grew warmer. "I knew you would not turn me away, Zendric. Your word confines you, just as steel chains hold a thief."

"You have given me no choice," Zendric said, slowly and seriously. "Do not think I have forgotten my debt to you. I would do anything to . . . " He paused as though contemplating the meaning of his next words.

And in that quiet, frozen moment, Driskoll sneezed.

A roar went up inside the window, and footsteps thundered toward the front door. "Who's there?" Zendric yelled.

The boys ran, skittering back away from the window and into the yard. Suddenly, Zendric was no longer behind them.

Instead, the angry wizard stood in the path before them, lowering his hands as though finishing a quick spell. Driskoll and Kellach skidded to a halt, their mouths gaping.

Zendric was clearly angry, his face flushed red.

"Curse it, Kellach! Listening at my window! I thought that your mother had raised you to know better."

"We . . . we wanted to wish you a Happy Promise Festival," Kellach said.

"By eavesdropping on my conversations?" Zendric looked down at Driskoll. "I see you weren't alone in this, lad. I'm disappointed—terribly disappointed in both of you." The old wizard clenched his hands against his dark blue robes.

"We didn't want to disturb you if you had a visitor. We saw the horse . . . " Driskoll blurted.

"We were doing our duty as Knights of the Silver Dragon," Kellach added. "We thought you were in trouble. We were protecting you—"

Zendric waved his hand angrily in front of them.

"I need neither protection nor courtesy," the old wizard snapped. "What I do need is an apprentice that I can trust. I expected more of you after we gave you the honor of becoming Knights of the Silver Dragon."

Both boys blanched. The old wizard's blue eyes were icy. "I do have a visitor but that is none of your concern."

Zendric stomped to the gate. He swung open the iron trellis, rocking back on his heels and fixing Kellach with a stern gaze. "Go on, lads. I have no time for more visitors today."

"But . . . what about my Promise gift—" Kellach began.

"Nor have I the time for idle amusements. If you are going to be a wizard someday, Kellach, you will have to learn that there are endeavors far more important than celebrations. Now leave me."

Kellach's shoulders slumped. He walked past the wizard, and back out into the road. Driskoll followed close behind.

As he closed the gate behind the boys, a touch of patience crept into Zendric's voice. "I know you were trying to help, and I thank you. Good day."

The wizard locked the gate and walked to his tower, never looking back.

With a sigh, Kellach turned away, shuffling his feet and pushing his hands into his pockets.

"Boy, that was rough," Driskoll said. "I'm surprised he didn't turn us both into toads. Still, I'd do anything to know who his visitor was." Driskoll followed his brother away from the tower, his hand absently on his new sword. "She wasn't from Curston, that's for sure. Did you see if she had a sword? Or a lute, maybe?"

"Cats," Kellach said absently, raising one hand to his chin.

"What are you talking about?"

"Cats. He prefers turning people into cats." Kellach stopped in the middle of the road. "Did you see his hand? Zendric had a mark on his hand."

"A mark?" Driskoll looked puzzled. "What, like a burn? Did he burn himself in his alchemy lab?"

"No, not like a burn. More like a bite. I saw it when we were in the yard. If I hadn't been so close, or if he hadn't been waving his hand around . . . "

Driskoll shrugged. "So what?"

Kellach looked back at the tower that glimmered through the trees behind them. Although he could no longer see the window where Zendric and his visitor were, he still turned the memory of their conversation over and over in his mind. Why did Zendric owe someone his life? And what was the woman forcing him to do to repay her?

"You know," Kellach said, half smiling. "Zendric's tower doesn't have any extra rooms for visitors."

"Sure," Driskoll replied. "His friend is probably staying in one of the inns on Visitor Street. Almost all of the inns in the city are there—all seven of them."

"Right. But most of them are family owned, and that means the innkeepers talk. A lot. Do you know how many rumors get started on Visitor Street? They might as well call it 'Whisper Street.' "

Kellach rubbed his chin thoughtfully. "There's no way Zendric would let his mystery guest stay in one of those places. There's only one inn in Curston known for its ability to keep the secrets of its residents."

"Oh no, Kellach. You're not thinking . . ."

"The Stein and Silence." Kellach turned and began running down the street.

"We can't!" Driskoll protested, but Kellach didn't turn around.

CHAPTER

4

"**G**et out and stay out!"

The shout from the Stein and Silence echoed through the street. A mean-looking wizard crashed through the door and skidded across the cobblestones.

Kellach and Driskoll stood in an alley several yards away from the infamous inn. The sun had begun to set and Visitor Street was full of people.

Kellach peered up and down the street, looking for any sign of their father. Torin definitely wouldn't be amused if he saw them standing here.

"Did you see that?" Driskoll choked. "We can't go in there!"

Kellach grabbed onto the steel torch sconce that hung from one of the stone walls and pulled himself up to see over the crowds in the street. "That's where the woman will be staying. It's where all the thieves stay. Everybody knows it."

"Exactly my point!" Driskoll tugged on Kellach's robes, trying to pull his older brother down from the vantage point. "Look, you know Dad told us never to go down there."

"I don't see Dad," Kellach called down. "But I do see a whole group of watchers in front of the Stein and Silence."

"Great."

"Don't be such a chicken, Driskoll." Kellach dropped lightly to his feet on the cobblestone. Completely ignoring his younger brother's protests, Kellach strode down the winding corridor, artfully stepping around the celebrants and grinning back at Driskoll. Left without a choice, Driskoll followed him.

Faint singing echoed along the street, drifting out from warm, music-laden inns. Torches burned every few feet, and groups of townsfolk pushed against each other in the cobblestone streets, making their way from one inn to the next.

People in Curston didn't normally go out in the evening. The streets were dangerous, and monsters roamed in the dark. But once a year at Promise Festival, the watch extended the curfew for one hour after sundown. Watchers lit all the torches and stood on every street corner in the Phoenix Quarter. People roamed though the quarter as they pleased. It was considered a return to the days of Promise, when nothing preyed upon the citizenry of this small town.

As the two boys worked their way toward the inn at the far end of the bustling street, Driskoll sighed. "First Breddo, then Zendric, and now my brother," he muttered. "All completely cracked."

"*Ssshh,* look!" Kellach said. "Here it is."

The sign that hung over the doorway of the Stein and Silence was crooked, its jagged wooden bottom showing signs of wear and soot from fire. The walls of the inn weren't any cleaner, covered in the dust of travel and in the dark stain of ash. A dark alley snaked along one side of the inn.

Both boys shaded their eyes and peered in the window.

Inside, a barmaid carried a heavy platter of ale mugs to a table. A bard strummed his harp and sang. The patrons laughed and cheered.

"The bard's playing 'The Warrior's Way,' " Driskoll said. He listened to the sweet sound of the bard's harp, a smile lighting his lips. "That's a good one for the Promise Festival. Full of mystery and heroism."

"I don't see Zendric's friend, do you?" Kellach asked.

Driskoll shook his head.

"Get off me!" a voice shouted.

The boys whirled around.

A pair of watchers were breaking up a small fight on the street, pulling two men apart despite their screaming insults. One of the two was clearly a practiced warrior. He wore black leather armor and a tight cap on his head. Roaring loudly, he tried to push the watchers away with a kick of his massive leg.

The other man—a wizard—shivered in the middle of the street. He drew the sleeve of his velvet cloak across his mouth to wipe away the blood on his lip.

"Keep away from me, you no-good bandit!" the wizard shouted. He didn't seem to notice that the bandit was more than twice his size.

The bandit growled and returned the wizard's insults with a string of curses.

Another man in black leather poked his head out of the inn's door. "Sir, come quickly," he shouted at the bandit. "We've found her!"

"Who are those black-armored guys?" Driskoll whispered.

"I'm not sure, but I'm guessing they're talking about Zendric's guest," Kellach said. "Come on. Let's get out of the way before they notice us."

The watchers held fast, but the warrior was too strong for them. He twisted sharply and broke their grip. Then he raced across the road.

The man in the street lifted a hand and chanted—strange words spilling out of his mouth like a fountain.

Kellach's eyes widened in surprise, and he began to run.

"Get down!" Kellach screamed, knocking his brother to the ground.

The man finished his spell and released a thick puff of wool from his hand. As the wool fell, a black tarry goo burst out of his fingers.

The bandit ducked into the inn's door just in time. The goo landed instead on the torches above the door and exploded into green flames.

The watchers yelled, and the wizard in the street stared in stunned amazement.

"It isn't supposed to do that," he murmured numbly, but his words were all but lost in the chaos that erupted along with the flames.

As the fire began to wrap itself around the building, the bouncers at the door gaped for a moment and then started screaming for help.

Watchers came running with buckets. The bouncers upended the inn's water trough onto the flames to try to prevent them from spreading. But the fire flickered like lightning down the sticky tendrils of tar.

"Driskoll, look!" Kellach grabbed his brother's arm, pointing down the dark alleyway alongside the inn.

A single figure, hooded and wrapped in velvet robes, darted out of a side exit. A second later, through the smoke, Kellach made out three forms giving chase. The light of the still-burning flames in the street glinted off steel: the pursuers were armed.

"How did she get here without us seeing her?" Driskoll's eyes were wide.

"The same way Zendric got in front of us at the tower—magic."

"She's a wizard?"

"Zendric is." Kellach pushed to his feet. "He probably teleported her here so she wouldn't be seen riding through the city."

And without another word, Kellach bounded across the street. He dodged the flames flickering off the inn's walls and entered the alley.

"Kellach, . . . wait . . . for me!" Driskoll called from behind his brother.

Kellach slowed to a jog and let Driskoll catch up with him.

"Come on! It's our only chance to find out what's going on." Kellach grabbed his brother's arm.

The alleyway divided, twisting back and dumping them out on the north end of Visitor Street, past the other inns and the small houses behind them.

The boys sped around the corner and caught sight of the woman grabbing the reins of a horse. Her face was hidden beneath her thick velvet hood. A fat pouch hung from a belt around her cape.

She threw her foot into the stirrup and dragged herself onto the horse. The three men surrounded her, knives flashing in their hands.

The horse reared, pulling away from the men and backing down the cobblestone street. One man reached to grip the horse's reins, twisting them cruelly. The steed reared higher and whinnied.

The woman kicked out, knocking the man to the ground. The second man sliced at her with his knife, with a sickening, tearing sound. She gripped her side as her belt tore away.

Her pouch fell to the ground, rolling and spinning along the cobblestones.

With a savage tug, the woman spun her horse around and spurred it down the street. The three men ran down the street after her, cursing.

Kellach darted out into the street and picked up the woman's pouch.

"Kellach, what are you doing?" Driskoll hissed.

"It's the only clue we—" Kellach began. He didn't have time to finish the thought.

The three men were back. Shoulders slumped, they plodded down the street toward the boys.

Kellach stood frozen. The pouch hung from his hand, the leather strap of the belt trailing to the ground in a long strip.

The men at the end of the street stopped and stared for a moment at Kellach and the pouch in his hand. One was a tall, lanky fellow. The second bandit was shorter, heavier, with solid muscles and red hair that kept falling in front of his eyes. The third, the man from the street fight, wore a tight cap on his head.

The man in the cap raised his knife and pointed it at Kellach.

"Drop that bag, boy," he snarled, the knife flashing in his hand.

Together, the three bandits, sneers on their lips, began to walk toward Kellach and Driskoll.

"Drop that bag," the redheaded man repeated, "and you might still live to see the dawn." The three bandits laughed.

"Kellach," Driskoll said, hand on the hilt of his new sword. "I don't think we can fight them."

As if he had heard Driskoll's whispered comment, the lanky bandit spun his knife expertly, his movements reflecting the true grace of a master bladesman.

"Quick! Cast a spell!" Driskoll blurted.

Kellach's blue eyes were clear and unafraid. "The minute I start casting, we'll be dead."

"One choice then . . ." Driskoll said as the two boys stepped backward in a single identical movement. "Run."

CHAPTER

5

Kellach and Driskoll plummeted down the side streets of Curston.

Kellach looked back over his shoulder as they rounded a corner, but the men in black leathers were steadily gaining. He stuffed the pouch beneath his robes. The cold lump nestled against his stomach.

The two boys ran through Main Square, darting among the crowds. People leaped back, startled.

"Watch where you're going!" a man shouted.

But Kellach and Driskoll didn't have time to apologize. They ran on, knocking over a barrel and scattering anything unlucky enough to be in their path.

"Maybe . . . we can . . . find Dad!" Driskoll gasped as he dodged past a startled tradeswoman.

"Follow me!" Kellach shouted.

The boys cut through a thin alleyway from Main Square to the warehouse area. Unlike the wide stone plaza of Main Square, the streets here were filled with tall wooden buildings standing in neat rows along randomly cornered streets. The boys rounded a corner in front of a tall, narrow warehouse with whitewashed doors.

Suddenly two of the bandits leaped out from behind a water trough, knocking the trough over and blocking the way down the street.

The bandits marched forward.

"You're trapped now, boys!" the lanky man snarled. "Give us the bag!"

Kellach raised his hand, trying to concentrate as Zendric had shown him.

Driskoll drew his sword, holding it warily before him.

The lanky bandit lunged forward and slashed at Driskoll. Driskoll blocked his strike with a halfhearted thrust. There was a loud ring as the blade of the knife skidded across Driskoll's steel. Driskoll stepped back.

He looked as startled as his attacker at the success of his block.

The bandit grinned. "You were lucky that time, boy. But not this time!"

As he moved in, Driskoll tucked his sword into his belt and resorted to the one thing he knew well—fighting with his brother. He kicked at the bandit's shin. The man shouted in pain and jumped back.

Meanwhile, the red-haired bandit darted around Driskoll. He lifted his knife preparing to plunge the weapon into Kellach's arm.

"Billeous luminum!" Kellach cried, making the gestures with one hand and drawing out a small lightning bug from his

own belt pouch with the other.

Instantly, a terrible, bright light illuminated the alley. Scintillating colors erupted from Kellach's palm, radiating outward in rainbows of incandescent light. The bandit grabbed his eyes, shouting in pain and stumbling backward.

Before the third man could catch up, the boys fled again. They scrambled over the trough and past the padlocked doors that lined the street.

"How long will that blind him?" Driskoll yelled.

Kellach shook his head. "Only a few seconds. We'd better get lucky."

"I keep telling you—I don't need luck." Driskoll gripped his sword with a grin, running at full tilt next to his brother. "I just . . . ," he panted, "need a sword!"

Kellach risked a glance backward. He saw the man in the cap had now rejoined his friends. He kicked the two men viciously, then pointed after the boys and yelled something unintelligible. Within seconds, the others had gotten to their feet and started running once more. The boys had only gained a few seconds— not enough to make their escape.

"They're trying to force us into a dead end," Kellach said.

"Dead end. Nice." Driskoll rolled his eyes. "It'll be a dead end, for certain, if they catch us!"

"Don't worry. I have a plan." As Kellach spoke, a thin knife flew a hairbreadth away from his head. Kellach ducked as the knife thudded into the wooden wall of a warehouse.

"Any time now, Kell!" Driskoll shouted.

Kellach skidded to a halt as they spun around another corner, suddenly realizing that they had fallen into an alley with no exits.

He looked behind them, gauging the distance to the other streets, only to see the bandits slowing down at the entrance to the alley, smiles on their brutish faces.

The three men grinned. As they exchanged eager glances, the man in the cap stepped forward, drawing a pair of long daggers from scabbards against his thighs. There was something familiar about the man, and Kellach paused to stare at him. The dagger wielder twisted his grip on the blades, with a strange, almost dreamlike grin on his face.

"Are we ready now, boys?" he said. The voice nagged Kellach's memory. "Or do we play chase some more?"

"If you've got any more useful spells, Kellach, you'd better use them now!" Driskoll hissed, trying to cover all their attackers with his blade.

"Look, Driskoll," Kellach tugged on his brother's sleeve and pointed up. "A window."

Driskoll looked. "I think magic has finally driven you insane. That window's more than fifteen feet up! Even if you stood on my shoulders, you'd never reach it, much less get through it."

"Don't worry, little brother." Kellach grinned. "I've got it covered." He began chanting, twisting his fingers in the air and reaching toward his belt pouch.

Even as he began, the bandits realized what he was doing and charged.

"Don't let that boy work his wizardry!" yelled the leader. He hurled another knife. The blade sailed directly toward Kellach.

"No!" Driskoll leaped in front of his brother. The dagger handle bounced off his shoulder and clattered to the ground. Driskoll shouted in pain.

The other two bandits charged. Driskoll set his feet, lifting his sword, with a desperate look on his face.

Then, suddenly, he was flying.

CHAPTER

6

Kellach and Driskoll flew upward, their feet leaving the ground as though gravity had lost its hold.

"Grab the ledge before we levitate too high!" Kellach reached for the window, and his fingers locked against the open shutters. Driskoll grabbed the other side with one hand still clinging to his sword.

"How long will this last?" he said, trying to pull himself through the open window.

"Only a few more seconds—quickly!"

The two boys floated through the opening into the warehouse. Kellach's stomach churned. The levitation spell was already fading. He could feel his body growing heavier.

Their arms and legs flailed helplessly as gravity wavered and then returned. With a yelp, Driskoll spun his body, landing roughly on his shoulder. "Ow!" he cried.

Kellach stood up, and tried to peer through the dim interior of the warehouse. "It won't be long before they find another way in." He rested his hand on the pouch hidden beneath his robes. "We've got to find a place to hide."

Kellach held out his hand and helped his younger brother stand. The warehouse was huge, filled with high stacks of crates and strange pillars wrapped in thick canvas covering. The floor was tidy, made of hard-packed dirt covered in a light layer of clean straw. The thick wooden beams across the ceiling threw crisscross shadows onto the ground. The two boys moved through the warehouse as silently as possible. Driskoll kept his sword low but ready for anything.

"That looks like a good spot," Kellach whispered. He pointed to the crack between two large stacks of crates in the darkest corner of the warehouse. Driskoll nodded.

The two boys crawled between the crates and waited.

From time to time, they heard footsteps in the warehouse, the movement of soft boots against the straw floor betraying their enemies' location. Several of the windows above them streamed moonlight into the interior, casting an eerie, glowing light on the stacks of crates in front of them.

"I'm almost out of spells," Kellach whispered. "If they find us, Driskoll, we've got a real problem. Maybe we should find another way out of the building."

"First we need to get into the warehouse. Now we need to get out of the warehouse." Driskoll rolled his eyes.

"I'm just trying to get us out of this mess."

"Yeah, the mess you got us into!"

"Well, if you weren't such a chicken . . ."

Driskoll's eyes narrowed. "I'm *not* a chicken!"

Just then, the boys heard the sound of the window above them shattering. Moonlight spilled across the crates, revealing the boys in their hiding place.

"I found them!" yelled the stocky, red-haired bandit.

Driskoll squirmed out of the crack. "You figure out a way to get out of here, Kellach! I'll hold them off!"

"Driskoll! No!" Kellach shouted. But it was too late.

Kellach watched helplessly as Driskoll turned to face the bandit, raising his new sword to the ready. The stocky, muscular man grinned, red hair falling into his eyes. He hardly slowed his pace as he charged with a long, thick dagger glinting in his hand. He obviously didn't think that the young boy would be much of a match.

Driskoll slashed wildly through the air. The bandit's knife came dangerously close to Driskoll's face.

Driskoll fell back, landing hard on the ground. His sword flew from his hand, landing three feet away. It skidded to a halt at the base of the large stack of crates.

"Driskoll, watch out!" Kellach dashed out from his hiding place.

The bandit jumped forward, the large knife in his hand striking low, like a cat's claw. Driskoll rolled along the ground to get away. The bandit's knife struck the ground.

"Hold still!" the black-armored man snarled.

Kellach spotted a broken board sticking out against the wall of the warehouse. He slammed it down on the bandit's head. The man cried out sharply, then went limp.

Driskoll squirmed out from under the unconscious man.

Kellach handed him his sword. "Gods, Driskoll. Are you insane?"

Driskoll set his chin. "I told you I wasn't a chicken."

"Yeah, you're just crazy." Kellach sighed. "Look, we've got

to find a way out of here." Kellach's head zipped back and forth. Behind a high stack of empty crates, he spotted a long strip of wood. He pushed aside the crates. A skinny ladder leaned against a balcony filled with more crates. Without stopping to think, Kellach climbed up the ladder.

From the top of the balcony, Kellach looked down. The tall, lanky bandit rounded the corner between the stacks of crates. He was headed straight for Driskoll.

"Kellach?" Driskoll yelled, fear making his voice quaver.

"Up here!" Kellach called. As he spoke he pushed a crate over the side of the balcony.

The lanky bandit barely had time to look up and realize that the crate was falling before it landed on him. Large and heavy, it landed with a crash, knocking the shocked bandit to the floor. The crate split open, and Kellach had a glimpse of straw pouring out over the bandit and his red-haired friend, burying them both in yellowy strands.

Driskoll looked up and flashed a grin at his brother. "Thanks!"

"Don't start celebrating yet," Kellach said as he climbed the ladder down to the warehouse floor. "That balcony leads nowhere. Just more storage space. And there's one more bandit still out there!"

A loud crash off to his right made Kellach spin around in surprise. A knife flew past his head. Kellach caught sight of the third bandit darting from shadow to shadow, fading into the darkness as he watched.

Kellach gritted his teeth and grabbed Driskoll's hand. He pulled his brother down the center aisle of the warehouse toward the main doors. "We're getting out of here."

"But what about the other bandit?" Driskoll asked.

44

"We'll just have to risk it."

As if on cue, the man in the tight cap emerged from behind a row of crates and charged toward them. Kellach's hands wove through the air in magical patterns. It was the last spell in his memory—really, hardly more than a cantrip, not very useful—but it was all he had.

The bandit growled. He slammed his shoulder into Kellach's ribs, lifting the knife for a savage jab to the boy's midsection.

In the same moment, Kellach's spell ended.

A burst of sulfur colored the air, and a small globe of fire appeared in Kellach's hand. The young wizard slapped his open palm against the bandit's face.

The man's eyebrows sizzled. Both Kellach and his attacker cried out in pain. The small globe of fire had blackened Kellach's hand as well as his enemy's face.

The bandit staggered backward, shaking his head to clear his eyes. He tripped and fell on his back with a loud thump.

Just then, a tremendous noise caught Kellach's attention. The large shipping doors to the warehouse swung open with a clatter. In the open doorway stood a troop of watchers, swords raised.

Bright torchlight illuminated everything around them. Kellach blinked, shielding his eyes from the sudden light. The watchers surrounded Driskoll, yelling for him to drop his sword. With a sigh of relief, Driskoll let the weapon slide from his hand.

Kellach grinned. "You're right on time. There are two bandits pinned under a crate at the back. And one right here—" Kellach pointed down.

But the bandit was gone.

CHAPTER

7

"Search the warehouse," Kellach called out. "He was right here just a second ago."

A few of the watchers stared at Kellach with suspicion, but one of them moved forward.

"Kellach?" The gruff voice was familiar. "Driskoll?"

"Gwinton!" Kellach called out, waving. The burly dwarf walked toward them, sheathing his double-edged axe. He was stocky, even for a dwarf, with a roll in his step that spoke of years of weapons practice. Gwinton's hair was thick, his beard tended with pride, and the axe at his side was worn from years of use. "What in the gods' darkest names are you doing here?"

Driskoll started to explain. "We were at Visitor Street, looking for—"

"We were looking for someone," Kellach cut in, "when we saw three men—bandits. They started chasing us and we hid here. Then they broke in after us."

"We dropped a crate on them," Driskoll added. "Well, Kellach did."

Kellach grinned. "We tried to find the watchers to help us, but I don't know where Dad is. He wasn't in Main Square."

"No, he's here. With us." Gwinton looked a bit uncertain, his round face wrinkling up with concern. "But, boys, Torin is—"

Just then, Torin's voice wafted through the doorway to the warehouse.

"I understand, sir. Nothing like this has ever happened before." Torin's usually deep voice sounded weak. "Please don't be mad, Arren. I know you're angry, but I can fix it."

A short man stormed into the warehouse, a blue vest flowing to his knees. He had brown hair, silvering with age, but his features were hawklike and sharp. Torin, his shoulders slumped, followed behind him.

"Captain," Arren scolded, "I must say I'm extremely upset by this. In this time of festival, I was assured that security would be of the utmost importance. My warehouse holds several irreplaceable treasures and many rare plants for my studies." His blue-gray eyes flashed with a commanding stare.

"Arren, sir, I'm really, really sorry." Torin glanced around, his eyes never seeming to fix on anything. "It should never have happened. There was a fire—an inn on fire—and . . . I don't understand how this could have happened . . . "

"That's your problem, not mine, Captain." Arren's voice was uncompromising. He swept past the boys, taking in Driskoll and Kellach's faces with a scowl.

"What are these?" Arren said, staring down at them.

"They . . . *uh* . . . they . . ." Torin stared at the boys openly, not quite certain of his answer. "They are children." He paused,

47

staring at them for another moment. Then he broke into a smile. "They are my children!"

"You should teach them better manners, Captain." Arren spun on one heel and marched into the back of the warehouse, his eyes counting every crate and shrouded item.

Torin's face fell, and he shuffled after Arren. Gwinton and the other watchers jogged behind him.

Kellach and Driskoll stared first at their father, then at each other.

"What in the gods was that?" Driskoll looked stunned. "He didn't even yell at us."

"I don't know, but I'm going to find out," Kellach said. "Come on." He grabbed Driskoll by the arm and marched after the men.

Gwinton stood in the corner of the warehouse, overseeing several watchers as they inspected the broken crate. Straw spewed out of the wooden slates, but no men lay pinned beneath it. The bandits were long gone—probably helped to escape by their third companion, Kellach realized.

By now, the three men would be lost among the city's populace, bruised and battered, but ready to continue their hunt for the boys. Kellach shivered. He thought back to the faces of their attackers. He was sure he knew these men—but from where?

A few yards away, Arren and Torin stood face to face. Arren's hawklike nose cut a stoic profile against Torin's firm jaw and narrow brown eyes.

"This was one of my most expensive pieces, and it has been positively treated like trash!" Arren shouted and pointed at the shattered crate.

48

"Who is that man?" Kellach asked Gwinton, eyes narrowing.

"Who? Him?" Gwinton shrugged. "Arren. He's an alchemist by trade. He's got a shop down on Paige Street. He owns this warehouse and rents out space to passing adventurers. I'd be amazed if he knows some of the crazy things they store in here before they're finished in those dungeons. He's also got a lot of friends. High-placed friends. You know, politics." The dwarf's beard waggled as he scowled. Gwinton lifted his shoulders slightly. "But, Arren's a good businessman, and a friendly fellow. Well, when he's not riled up like he is now."

"That statue is priceless!" Arren's voice cut through Gwinton's explanation, anger resonating in every tone. "It is part of a matching set with the one given to the city. Absolutely irreplaceable!"

Kellach looked into the broken crate. Inside, half hidden by the piles of packing straw, was a tall statue. It was carved from expensive-looking marble, the features and clothing exquisitely sculpted by a master's hand. The form was of a young man, around sixteen or seventeen years old, wearing the uniform of a young watcher. His face registered a look of mild surprise or fascination. A deck of cards arched in the midst of shuffling between his widespread hands. The marble arch between his hands was masterfully done. Kellach could almost hear the sound of shuffling cards as he looked at the incredible detail of the work.

"Arren, I see the statue." Torin continued eagerly. "It's pretty. Very pretty. The kids played with the statue, but they didn't break anything."

Arren shot Torin a fierce look, and the captain shivered, eyes widening as if he had been scolded. "I'm sorry . . . "

Kellach stared in horror. Was this really his father?

Arren pointed a bony finger in Torin's face, demanding, "You will take personal responsibility, Captain, if this or any other piece of work in this warehouse is harmed.

"I take pride in the security of my warehouse. I keep my own materials here as well as renting out space, and I reserve certain sections purely for alchemy supplies. But this is the second time someone's broken in here in the past week. I won't stand for it."

Finally noticing the boys, Arren pointed his accusatory finger at Driskoll and Kellach. "What if these wretched little boys of yours had set something on fire? The warehouse district might have been in jeopardy!"

"But . . . boys?" Torin tilted his head. " Boys! What are you doing here? I'm so happy to see you! Are you having fun at the festival?" He looked at Kellach's singed hand.

"Aw, Kellach. You got a boo-boo." Torin grinned lopsidedly.

Torin shook his head, then looked back down at them and ruffled Driskoll's damp hair. "Hope you liked your sword, Driskoll. Promise Gift. I wanted to get you something nice."

"Dad—" Kellach began, but Arren cut him off.

"That . . . boy is Zendric's apprentice, isn't he?" Arren jabbed his finger at Kellach. "I bet he tried to break into my warehouse to steal from me!"

Torin hid his face in his hands and said nothing.

"Zendric's always trying steal to my spells and herbs," Arren continued. "I bet Zendric's been sending these children as thieves! Did he tell you to come here?"

Arren stomped toward Kellach, his fingers clenched like a

bird's extended talons as he snarled, "You can tell Zendric he's not welcome in my warehouse, and he's not welcome in my shop!"

Kellach bristled. "Don't you blame anything on Zendric. He had nothing to do with this!" But even as he said it, an image of the woman at Zendric's window flashed into his mind.

Arren stood directly in Kellach's path, the tall youth's face only inches from the reddened pallor of the angry alchemist.

Arren's voice was a whisper too faint for the watchers to hear. "You tell your master that he'll find no wyrmserum here, you wretched little child."

Kellach instinctively took half a step back.

"Now get out," Arren finished with a shout. "Get them out of my warehouse!"

Torin nodded mutely. He walked toward the boys, making shooing motions toward the warehouse door.

Kellach and Driskoll scurried backward.

"We didn't do anything, Dad. We were attacked," Kellach began.

"I don't care," Torin said. He stared at the boys, but his eyes seemed vacant. He stopped and stood for a long minute, mouth open and hands hanging at his sides.

And then, for a moment, it seemed as if Torin was his old self. He clapped Gwinton on the shoulder. "Gwinton, please see my boys to the door."

In the distance, Arren let out a shout of anger, and Torin almost jumped out of his skin.

"Uh-oh." Torin frowned. "I think I have to do my job now. Did you hear? There's been a break-in . . ." Torin jogged back to the broken crate.

The dwarf escorted Kellach and Driskoll to the door, talking as they walked. "Torin's acting a little weird today. It started just a little while after lunch. He had a meeting with that wizard fellow, Zendric. I think it's been hanging over him all day. Zendric was looking for some guest of his—someone who's here for the festival, I think. Torin's overworked from the festival, you know. Robberies all day, Pralthamus on his back at the opening ceremony, then this.

"Don't worry about him. He'll be more himself after a bit of sleep." As they reached the door, Gwinton patted Kellach on the shoulder and forced a grin to his roughened, sunburned face. "You boys should go home now."

"Thanks, Gwinton," Kellach said. "You're probably right. Dad'll be fine."

The two boys waved at Gwinton and then hustled through the warehouse doors.

"Do you really think Dad's okay?" Driskoll asked as they left the warehouse behind.

"No, he's definitely not okay." Kellach said. "And if we don't find out why, I have a feeling that the whole city's going to be in danger."

CHAPTER

8

Bang! Bang! Bang!

The pounding sound at the front door roused Kellach from his slumber, tumbling him awake right in the middle of a peaceful dream.

He stared groggily over at his brother. Driskoll lay facedown on his small cot, his hand stretched over the edge of his bed to rest upon the scabbard of his new sword. A faint snore erupted from beneath the blankets. Driskoll was fast asleep.

Kellach threw on his robes and stumbled down the stairs. The door shook under the eager knocking.

"Kellach! Driskoll!" Moyra's voice was muffled. Kellach groaned, then pulled open the door.

"Good morning, Moyra."

"Let me in," she pushed past him, her face worried. "The rumors are all over the city by now. You were in a fight? Are you all right?" Moyra inspected Kellach with her eyes, looking for any sign of blood.

He held up his hands, chuckling. "I'm fine, I'm fine."

"Where's your dad?" Moyra asked, her voice calmer now.

"I don't know. I don't think he came home last night." Kellach sighed and sat at the kitchen table, rubbing his weary eyes. "He was acting really weird yesterday."

"Weird how?" Moyra sat across from him, her red hair a mop of tangled waves on top her cherubic face. "Like Daddy?"

"Yeah, now that you mention it," Kellach said thoughtfully, "like Breddo. He was talking strangely. His speech was slurred, and he was kind of distracted. He kept repeating things. It was like he had cotton between his ears." Kellach looked into Moyra's green eyes and pondered. "But that's not the only strange thing. After we dropped you and your dad off, we went by Zendric's tower. He had a visitor. A woman. We figured she must be staying at the Stein and Silence so we went there—"

"The Stein and Silence?" Moyra yelped. "How could you go there without me! That place is dangerous!"

"We were in a hurry, Moyra. That woman is important, and we had to find out why." Kellach's mind kept turning to the night before. Who was that woman? Why was she in Zendric's tower, and what was wrong with Breddo and Torin?

Driskoll's cheery hello from the stairs made them both look up at him: still half asleep, his brown hair stuck out every which way. Although he'd barely pulled on a tunic and breeches, he still had his new sword in his hand and was buckling his scabbard to his side with a practiced efficiency.

"Morning, Moyra!" He grinned. "Kellach told you about the warehouse yet?

"Not yet," Moyra said.

Driskoll filled her in on everything that had happened: the

hooded woman, the bandits, the chase in the warehouse, and Arren—adding lots of heroic flourishes.

Moyra's lips twitched into a smile. "I'm glad you two are all right!" she said. "But what does it all have to do with Zendric? And my dad?"

"Zendric said something at his tower. Wyrmserum," Kellach remembered. "Arren said it too. He accused me of trying to steal it for Zendric." Kellach got up and pulled a book from the bookshelf, digging through it for information.

"What are you looking up?" Driskoll asked.

"My index of spell components," Kellach explained.

As Kellach thumbed through the book, Driskoll turned to Moyra. "I'm sorry we didn't get a chance to talk to Dad about Breddo."

"I understand," Moyra replied. "It doesn't sound like he would have been much help anyway." She sighed, placing her head in her hands and propping her elbows on the table. "My dad's still sleeping. I had the old lady who lives next door keep an eye on him. All she ever does is peer in through the window. She might as well be useful while she's spying on us."

"Hey. Look what I found out about wyrmserum." Kellach opened his book and showed them the entry in the index.

"Wyrmserum," he read aloud. "A rare liquid compound used in spells of mind control." Kellach looked up. "Mind control! Of course."

Moyra sat up straight in her chair. "Maybe that's what's wrong with my dad and Torin. Someone is using a mind control potion on them."

"Someone like Zendric?" Driskoll added.

Kellach sat down at the table. "Perhaps a wizard. But I doubt Zendric is behind this."

"If not Zendric, then who? I mean, we've got to start looking at the facts." Driskoll began to count on his fingers. "First, Breddo and Torin are acting funny. They're confused, they're forgetting things, and they're acting totally creepy. Like they're under some kind of mind control. Second, Zendric mentioned this wyrmserum, this mind-control spell. We heard it ourselves! Third, all the mind-control victims were visited by Zendric before they went nuts. Remember? Guffy said Zendric came to visit the prison. And Gwinton said Zendric met with Dad! Maybe Zendric is using mind control on the people of Curston so he can take over the town."

"If Zendric were trying to take over the town," Kellach interrupted, "then why didn't he do something before now?"

"He's right," Moyra said. "Zendric's lived here a long time, and he's never shown any kind of ambition beyond warm tea and weird research."

"I think it's because he owes that woman," Driskoll said. "Remember what Zendric said when she was in his tower? 'You have given me no choice.' "

Moyra thumped her fist on the table. "She's making him do it. It's blackmail."

"Hey, maybe we can prove it!" Driskoll elbowed Moyra with excitement. "We have a clue we've forgotten about. Kellach, what happened to the pouch that fell off of the woman's belt?"

"Gods! I had completely forgotten. Let me get it." Kellach darted back toward the bedroom that the boys shared, picking up his other set of robes and the bag beneath it. He walked into the kitchen and set the pouch on the table in front of Moyra and Driskoll.

Kellach worked the knots free, untying the pouch's tight lacings and letting it fall open against the kitchen table. Once the leather had fallen away, they found a thick wrapping of silk scarves. Driskoll pulled at the fabric, unraveling at least three layers of thin, soft, red and purple cloth to reveal the inner treasure: a sphere no larger than his fist.

"It's just a metal ball," Driskoll said.

"More like a steel egg," Moyra took the sphere from Driskoll. Indeed, it was ovoid, its metal sides shining in the morning sunlight that filtered through their kitchen window. There were light tracings along the shell of the egg, spiraling and weaving in an intricate knotwork. "I wonder what's inside," she said.

"I don't see any way to open it," Kellach peered at the ball, running his finger over the etchings. "But, hang on." He took the egg from Moyra, carrying it to the window and looking carefully at the marks. "These markings are a wizard's seal. The egg must be some kind of a puzzle."

"A puzzle?" Moyra and Driskoll looked at each other.

"Yeah," Kellach chuckled, his mind already working on the delicate whorls and twists of the egg. Swiftly, his fingers began to trace the etchings, seeking any sign of a hinge or pin. Nothing. His fingers pressed every faint indentation and slid along the edges of the delicate engraving, seeking any kind of lever or moving part. A piece moved beneath his touch, and Kellach focused on it.

Bit by bit, Kellach worked the puzzle, feeling small pieces of scale shift into place as the picture on the silver shell of the

57

egg-shaped ball began to take form. The curves became rivers and the trails became the outline of a scaled dragon twisted into a ball. It was a striking resemblance. The lifelike talons carved into the steel shell looked almost as if they could move on their own. Then, suddenly, they did.

"I GOT IT!" Kellach jumped away from the window, his hands cupped around the steel egg and his eyes bright with success.

Indeed, the egg was moving in Kellach's hands. The etchings seemed alive, twisting and turning in his hand. Driskoll and Moyra stood up from their seats eagerly as Kellach placed his treasure on the tabletop. All three leaned forward to see what would erupt from the steel orb.

The etchings that covered the egg in tracings of black and gold shimmered and changed, becoming a faintly etched pattern of scales. The orb twisted, its steel sides suddenly shivering apart in long strips. As the three kids watched in awe, the upper sides of the egg broke apart into paired triangles. They stretched up and away from the body of the egg, revealing what was beneath—a stunning silver dragon figurine, about the size of a small falcon, with eyes that blazed in hues of violet.

"Wow, that's amazing," Kellach whispered.

"It's beautiful," Moyra said.

And then, the statue moved.

CHAPTER

9

Driskoll yelled and leaped away from the table.

The little dragon's wings spread more widely, its wedge-shaped head twisting up from its body on a long, elegant neck that shone with silver scales. Purple eyes blinked, and its mouth opened in a delicate yawn as its tail flashed out across the kitchen table.

"That thing's alive!" Driskoll's eyes were like saucers. Moyra covered her mouth with her hands.

"Actually, it isn't." Kellach said. "It's a machine. Look at it! It moves with perfect mechanical precision."

As the silver dragonet twisted its head to look up at them, they could hear the faint whir and click of gears. The creature hobbled across the table, wings extended to either side for balance. Its long tail coiled and lashed behind it. It extended a taloned paw, the claws wrapping loosely around Kellach's forefinger.

"Look at him," Kellach said.

"How do you know it's a him?" Moyra asked curiously.

"It just looks like a 'him,' " Kellach responded. "Doesn't he?

I think he understands me." The little dragon peered up at Kellach and made a soft chirrup of welcome.

"I don't know, Kellach," Moyra said. "It's just a machine."

"Kell-ak." The little dragon bobbed his head, violet eyes twinkling as his metal jaw struggled to replicate the word. He erupted in a whir of sound, chittering out the noise once more, "Kell-ak?"

"He can talk too?" Driskoll reached out to pet the smooth silver wings. "Is he magical, Kellach?"

"He must be. I've never seen anything like it," his brother responded.

Moyra's voice was openly skeptical. "I doubt anyone has—but that doesn't change the fact that it belongs to that woman. You remember, the one who's blackmailing Zendric? Or have you both forgotten about that?"

Just then, the dragon's claw tightened around Kellach's finger, sharp claws drawing a pinprick of blood from the young wizard's hand.

"Ow!" Kellach yelped, jerking his hand back as the dragonet's claw retracted. Suddenly, with a faint flash of violet light, the little dragon roared. The sound was tinny and indistinct, but it held the ring of magic.

"Ow," Kellach repeated weakly, his eyes captured by the dragonet's suddenly intense gaze.

The dragonet chirruped again, his gears whirring within his long throat.

"Kellach!" Moyra reached for his hand, checking to see if the wound was a deep one.

"It's nothing. Just a scratch. He says he's sorry."

Moyra and Driskoll stared at each other. "Hang on. Did you say he said something?" Driskoll asked.

"Couldn't you hear him?"

"I heard a bunch of noise. But it didn't make any sense." Staring again at the dragon, Driskoll tried to make sense of the whirring and clicking tones. "I think that's a word . . . maybe. It doesn't sound much like the common tongue."

"I don't know what language it is either. But somehow I can understand him." The silver dragon climbed up Kellach's sleeve, placing his claws delicately on Kellach's shoulder. He extended a shimmering neck to stare into his eyes. The whir and click turned into a purring sound. "He says that now we're bonded. I don't know what that means."

Kellach listened to the little creature as he chattered, nodding in understanding as the dragonet talked. "He's a clockwork dragon. He says he was made to be a wizard's familiar—designed to bond with one owner."

"Does he know any spells?" Driskoll asked.

Kellach laughed. "I doubt it. He doesn't even know where he is. Apparently, he wasn't supposed to be opened yet. I guess when I opened the egg, I triggered him. And now he's mine."

"Does it have a name?" Moyra's voice was skeptical.

"Lochinvar," Kellach translated the strange noises that came from the small silver creature. "He says his name is Lochinvar, and he wants to know why you're staring at him like that."

Kellach laughed as the dragonet scrambled up his shoulder. The creature tried to gain a hold without sinking his claws into Kellach's flesh, but managed only to look very much like a kitten, stranded on a tree limb.

"Kellach, we don't know who that woman is—or what she's holding over Zendric. Can we really trust this . . . thing?"

"Aw, come on, Moyra." Kellach held out his hands, and the dragon responded in kind, stretching his wings high over Kellach's head. "Look at him! How could he be involved?"

"That woman had it. She brought it to town for a reason. Until we know what that reason is, we have to assume this creature still works for her. And that means it—I mean he—is dangerous. We should make him roll back up, or whatever, and keep him in a sack until this is over with. What if this dragon is involved in the mind control that's affecting Breddo and Torin?"

"You're kidding, right?" Driskoll was completely enchanted by the silvery creature, watching as the little beast flapped his wings. "Think how useful he could be! And if Kellach can talk to him, he could carry messages or spy on people for us."

"That's exactly what I'm afraid of." Moyra crossed her arms belligerently. "We can't understand what he's saying. What if he tells that woman everything we say and do?"

"Then we'll have to keep him with us," Kellach said. "Maybe he knows stuff about her too. Did you think of that?"

Both Moyra and Driskoll looked at Kellach, who turned to the dragon. He was now petting the boy's face with his shining head, purring in a low undertone. Kellach caught his amethyst eyes and said, "What do you know, Lochinvar? About before . . . before you were out of the egg? What do you remember?"

The little clockwork creature sat up on its haunches, gibbering in broken phrases and chittering metal clicks.

"He says," Kellach translated, "that it was very hot and very strange and, then, very dark. For a long time. And then I opened the egg, and he thinks I'm wonderful." Kellach chuckled. "He's not a lot of help, I'm afraid."

Moyra frowned, shaking her head so that her red hair flew. "No, he's not. And I think you should put him back in that pouch."

"We should put it to a Silver Dragon vote." Kellach looked seriously at the other two. "All those in favor of letting Locky stay?" Kellach raised his hand, and Driskoll's quickly followed.

"All those opposed?"

Moyra's hand grudgingly lifted into the air. She scowled and sat back down in the kitchen chair with a sigh of exasperation.

"Fine, but this little dragon still doesn't solve our problem. What are we going to do about my dad? And your dad? We have to help them."

Kellach sat back down at the table and propped up the index of spell components once again. Locky peered over his shoulder as Kellach reread the index entry on wyrmserum, puzzling over the implications.

"Like any serum," Kellach said, "this potion is made of several items, the same way that a cake is made of flour, eggs, and other ingredients. It's a compound. Maybe if we knew what is in it, we could make an antidote."

He ran his finger over the entry. "For ingredients, see *Serums, Potions, and Elixirs.*" Kellach looked up. "I don't have that book."

"Didn't you say it's rare? Whatever's in wyrmserum, it can't be easy to find." Driskoll clicked his tongue against his teeth as he thought. "Wyrm. That means snake, right, Kellach? Well, maybe it's made from a snake, then. Or a magic serpent!"

"Calm down, Driskoll. If a magic serpent lived anywhere

near Curston, the watch would have heard of it." Kellach poked his head back into the book. "We've got to think about this logically if we're going to get anywhere."

"Remember what my dad said before he collapsed?" Moyra said. "He was ranting about the prison and the cell at the end of the corridor, whatever that means."

Kellach's head popped out of the book. "You're right! Whoever poisoned your dad did it in the prison. Watchers are missing, and prisoners and the captain of the watch are going nuts. Everything leads back to the prison and Watchers' Hall." Kellach closed the book, getting to his feet and planting his fists on the table. "I say we go back there and find out what's going on."

Locky twisted his head toward Kellach and gave a victorious little chirrup.

"No way," Driskoll said. "Remember the last time we tried to break into the prison? I'm not putting poor Guffy through that again."

"There are other ways of getting into the prison. Secret ways," Moyra said.

"What?" Driskoll said. "Moyra, are you saying that all this time you've known a secret way into the prison, and you didn't tell us?"

Moyra shrugged. "You never asked."

Driskoll gawked at her.

Moyra ignored him. "There's a small network of tunnels running beneath Watchers' Hall. Breddo told me about them. I've been through only once. A couple of years ago, I tried to help my dad take a . . . *ahem* . . . a break from his sentence. But the tunnels are too small for him to fit through."

Moyra glanced up and down at the boys, sizing them up. "I think we could all squeeze through just fine."

Driskoll continued to stare at her.

Moyra blushed, her face turning as red as her hair. "Cut it out."

She lifted her sharp chin in defiance. "There's something in that prison that hurt my father's mind. We need to find out what it was. All in favor?"

All three kids raised their hands. Even the little dragonet lifted one leg.

Moyra looked at Locky and scowled. "But I'll warn you—if you're dead-set on bringing that creature along, you'd better teach him to be quiet. Things echo when they're underground, and where we're going, we can't afford to make noise."

10

I don't know why I have to carry the sack," Driskoll complained, hefting the bag to his shoulder.

"We're going to need the sack," Moyra explained. She climbed over the wall of a burned-out building in Broken Town. "Just trust me on this one. Okay?"

Moyra held out her hand and helped Driskoll and Kellach over the wall.

"Watch out!" Moyra pointed out shards of old, broken glass. Dandelions covered a faint patch of grass that grew within the ruined building. In the distance, through the building's tattered shell, they could see the back of Watchers' Hall.

Driskoll shivered. "Isn't this near where that other watcher disappeared?"

"This is the area he patrolled," Kellach said, petting the dragon on his shoulder with a gentle hand. "But no one knows exactly where he disappeared."

They could hear echoes of the bright music of a festival day somewhere far away within the city.

"Second day of the Promise Festival," Driskoll said. "And we're spending it slogging through the dirt." He watched the banners unfurling in the morning breeze and let out a deep sigh.

"Here it is!" Moyra's voice sang out. "I found it!" She stood beside a large rock on the edge of the building and waved her hand toward them.

As Kellach and Driskoll approached, Moyra pushed the rock away, revealing a metal door in the ground.

"My dad said this used to be some kind of storage area," Moyra said as she pulled up the rusting door. "It was abandoned years and years ago, back when Watchers' Hall was first built. My dad used to play here as a boy. But the tunnels are too small for most adults to crawl through."

Kellach peered into the long, dark passage beneath the cellar door. Every few seconds, a bit of loose dirt fell to the tunnel floor. Spiders crawled all along the wall.

"Spiders! Oh great!" Driskoll said. "Are you sure this is safe?"

"Don't worry, silly," Moyra took the sack from him and knelt to open it.

"Are you sure this tunnel leads to the prison?" the skepticism in Driskoll's voice was obvious, and when both Kellach and Moyra stared at him disapprovingly, he flushed deeply.

"It takes us right under Watchers' Hall, near the cells." Moyra sighed, frustrated. "Now, are we heading for the prison, or are you going to stand here and be a coward about it?"

In answer, Driskoll fell to his knees beside her, helping her open the sack. "Here. I lugged it this far. I'll get it open." He twisted the sturdy knots with his fingers, untying the bag.

Inside were three lanterns with flint and steel, rope, a long knife, and an oilskin bundle that Moyra picked up and stuffed beneath her belt. "That's for me. It's my dad's." She crawled into the tunnel, squatting to avoid striking her head on the ceiling.

Driskoll sparked the flint and steel together, lighting one of the lanterns. "I'm glad you thought to bring these."

"If I hadn't, we'd be traveling in the dark." Moyra thumbed in Kellach's direction.

"Hey, what's that supposed to mean?" Kellach and Locky both peered at Moyra.

"Oh nothing. Just that you're too taken with that toy of yours to think straight."

"Do you really think Locky's dangerous? You're not dangerous, Locky, are you?" Kellach petted Locky's head and smiled.

"He is cute," Driskoll said.

Moyra rolled her eyes.

"Right." Moyra reached to take one of the lanterns. "Now, come on, let's get started." Moyra dropped down into the hole with Kellach and Driskoll right behind her.

"This tunnel isn't going to stay this size all the way to the prison, is it?" Clutching his sword, Driskoll eyed the cramped corridor warily.

"Nope." She smiled. "It gets smaller about halfway through."

The corridor twisted underground, forcing the three kids to crawl through the passage at a hobble. The deeper they moved into the tunnel, the colder it seemed to get. The air stank like a musty basement.

Moyra was first, pushing the lantern along in front of her

as she slipped easily between the thick corridors of stone and earth.

The boys were not as used to such tight places.

"Ow!" Driskoll yelped as he scraped his elbows on the rock. The passage had narrowed to a thin crack through the stone, and he, the roundest of the three, was forced to slink along on his stomach.

"I told you it was narrow." Moyra grinned back over her shoulder.

Driskoll stuck his tongue out at her. His protest would have been stronger if he hadn't found himself jammed against the wall of the small tunnel. "Um, Kellach? Can you push me?"

From the rear, Kellach grunted and pushed against the soles of his brother's boots until Driskoll was freed. Moyra stopped and considered their path, staring down pairs of seemingly endless corridors and tapping her teeth with her fingernail until she decided which way to go. At last, she tsk-tsked herself for forgetting and headed confidently down the right-hand path.

After what seemed like forever, Moyra came to a stop. "Here we are." The tunnel opened out onto a ledge just wide enough for the three of them to lie shoulder to shoulder on the stone. On the far side of the ledge was an iron grate.

Moyra slid forward onto the ledge until she could touch the iron grate. "Perfect. No lock. Looks like the watchers still haven't found the passage." She pushed the grate open and crawled into the hallway beyond. Quickly, she looked both ways down the dusty corridor.

"Nobody," she whispered. "Still, we'd better hurry. These corridors echo like crazy, and even though a watcher hasn't found us yet, that doesn't mean that someone hasn't heard the noise."

The dragon on Kellach's shoulder let out a curious whistle as the boy slid down from the ledge into the corridor.

"*Sssh,*" Kellach covered the dragonet's muzzle, shaking his finger at the little creature. "You have to be quiet now, Lochinvar," he murmured.

Wriggling, the dragonet spread his wings and beat them silently against the air as if in agreement. Kellach drew his hand away and the silver beast rubbed his wedge-shaped head against Kellach's cheek. "He says he can be quiet."

"He'd better," Moyra glowered as she took Driskoll's lantern so that he could climb through the open grate. "Or that dragonet is going to find himself on the scrap heap."

Driskoll gingerly squeezed through the small opening into the stone corridor beyond.

"Don't listen to her, Locky," Kellach petted the dragon on his shoulder. "Moyra really does like you." He ignored the girl's scowl and followed her through the corridor.

The passages deep in Curston's prison were dimly lit, and only a few flickering torches hung in the sconces along the stone walls. The corridors echoed, and the sound of every footfall seemed like a cannon in the gloomy underground. Although the walls were carved stone, they were shaped and mortared for solidity. Kellach touched the stone, feeling the smooth texture and imagining the keep above him.

Moyra led the boys through corridors that turned at right angles, pausing from time to time to peer into a cell door. The doors were solid oak, banded with iron straps that had been bolted to the wooden planks. There were two metal grates in each door:

one at the top for tall humans, elves, and other creatures and one nearer to the bottom for dwarves, halflings, and gnomes.

For the most part, the cells were empty, and the doors were open as though waiting for their next resident. Within each cell, Kellach and Driskoll could see a clean straw cot covered in modest linen, a washbasin and a water pitcher, and a tall chamber pot. The cells had stone floors and were covered with molding hay.

"Can the prison guards see us?" Driskoll asked. He peered around the corner, trying to gauge the distance of the next corridor in the gloom. "Should we cover our lanterns?" he asked as an afterthought.

"No need," Moyra shrugged, stepping ahead and checking the corridor for recent footprints. "If the guards only see the light, they'll assume that it's another guard making the rounds. They can hear us long before they can see us, and an echo is a lot more obvious than a lantern in this place."

Driskoll gulped, nodding. Moyra stepped ahead, checking inside a cell. She indicated that there was no prisoner inside, and the trio kept moving through the dark depths of stone.

"This is the area where my father was usually kept—it's the main prison. There are about twenty-six cells on each level, and usually only eight or nine of them are full at any time." Moyra kept her voice hushed, barely audible. Driskoll and Kellach, unused to the need for silence, simply nodded in understanding.

"There's another level, beneath this one. Supposedly, that's where they keep prisoners who are to be hanged."

Driskoll couldn't help but ask, "Hanged?"

Moyra nodded. "Oh, no one's been hung in Curston for years, but that's what it was built for. Gult mentioned that my dad was 'in the deep now.' " Moyra mockingly imitated the sergeant's voice. "I'll bet that means he was put on the lower level. If my dad saw anything, that's where it happened. Nobody ever really goes down there, so it's cut off from most of the traffic in the prison."

A coiled set of stone stairs led down from the cellblock, and Moyra stepped onto the first one with a faint hesitancy. "I've never been down here," she whispered, looking over her shoulder to be sure that Gult and the other guards weren't nearby. "We're going blind at this point."

"Wait!" Kellach squatted to look at the stairs carefully. "Moyra, you said that nobody uses these stairs, or the cells below them, right?"

Moyra nodded. "As far as I know, my dad's the only prisoner that's been held down there in the last few years." Her face stiffened as she thought of her father, and she looked away.

"There are footprints here—weird ones." Kellach pointed out the outline of shoes in the dust. "Breddo had leather boots. Here are Gult's footprints, hard-soled boots. There are some others, also boots, and probably watchers. But these are weird. They were made by slippers—soft ones, and very small. I'd say feminine."

Kellach peered closer and pinched his thumb and forefinger together, picking something off the floor. He stared at his fingers intently. "Strange," he murmured.

"What is it?" Driskoll asked.

Kellach held his fingers out. Driskoll and Moyra leaned in to see.

"Aw, it's just a thread," Driskoll said.

73

"Yes, but this thread's not made of normal material. It's more supple." Kellach rolled the piece of thread between his fingers. "Silk, maybe, or some other delicate weave. This did not come from the watchers' uniforms."

"It must be from that woman," Driskoll said. "Zendric's friend. You said that thread was made of silk, right? The kind of silk that people who wear velvet robes would have?"

"It's a stretch," Kellach whispered as they began moving down the circular stairs. "But, yes, it's possible. Here's the funny thing, though; the footprints aren't going down. They're coming up." Kellach paused and studied the stone more carefully.

"So the woman could have escaped from the cells?"

"If she did," Moyra said very softly, a touch of annoyance in her voice, "Then I doubt she'd have been wearing velvet."

"Good one," Driskoll said eagerly. He would have said more, but Moyra turned around and shushed him.

Driskoll smiled sheepishly, and placed his hand on his sword hilt as though to say he was ready.

They stepped into the lower corridor after three full revolutions of the stone steps. The passages here were narrower, and no torches lit the walls. Iron sconces hung empty against the stone. Moyra opened her lantern a bit wider and peered down the tunnel.

Kellach touched the stone, realizing that these passages were older than those above. "Moyra," he whispered, "this doesn't look like the Watchers' Hall stonework. It's more like the tunnels where we came in."

She looked carefully, and nodded. "Maybe they didn't do a lot of work here. I mean, if the passage already existed, then the builders would only have had to widen it. Less work for them."

The corridor was short, and Kellach could see only six oak doors, three to either side of the passage, and a sturdy iron door at the very end of the hall.

Rats scurried into the shadowy corners of the cells, crawling through remnants of hay and rock. The cots within the cells were hardly more than hammocks stretched from hooks in the walls that looked as though they might once have held manacles.

Moyra paused at the doorway to one cell, her breath catching in her throat. "I know that mark." She pointed at a carving on the inner side of the oak door. The wood had been carefully chiseled away, probably by a fork or other eating utensil.

"It's a *B*." Driskoll bent down to run his fingers over the wood. "For Breddo?"

Moyra nodded, her eyes growing hard. "He used to mark the doors of all the cells he's been in with that so he knows where he's been. There are about six cells like that up in the top level, all with his mark on the doors."

"So this is where Breddo was kept." As he knelt beside his brother, Kellach kept glancing at the floor on the outside of the doorway. "And look, more footprints. The slippers, again. It looks like they start behind that door." Kellach pointed at the iron portal that stood at the far end of the corridor.

Driskoll gasped. "The cell at the end of the corridor, just like Breddo said."

Kellach nodded and slipped down the corridor carefully, glancing back as Moyra and Driskoll followed. Indeed, the small, feminine footprints seemed to lead backward to the large metal door, vanishing beneath and into the chamber.

"Moyra, can you open this?" Kellach asked.

"What, that?" She stared at the huge piece of iron skeptically. "Well, maybe, Kellach. But it doesn't look friendly. What if that's the cell where they keep the psychopathic killers, like . . . Lexos?" She shivered.

"We've got to see what's behind there."

Driskoll pressed his ear to the door. "It doesn't sound like anyone's in there."

"Oh, all right." Moyra glanced back at the dark stairwell on the far end of the corridor. "Just keep your voice down, would you?"

Moyra approached the lock on the iron door as though it were a snake, keeping her hands away from the keyhole until she had taken a steady look. She motioned for Driskoll to hold his lantern closer, slanting the light so that she could get a better view. "This isn't a normal prison lock," she said doubtfully. "It's much sturdier. And that's saying something."

"Can you do it?" Kellach put his hands on his knees, leaning down to whisper next to her. The little dragonet slipped down his arm, hanging on with his claws and blinking his wide, amethyst eyes.

Moyra hardly spared the little creature a glance, but Kellach set Lochinvar down on the ground, placing a finger over his lips to remind the dragonet to keep silent.

Moyra lifted two of her father's tools and breathed deeply. She scowled in concentration and placed the first tool within the keyhole, sliding the second one along its length until she reached the first tumbler. Kellach watched intently, his eyes taking in every small and subtle movement of the tools.

Driskoll sat, cross-legged, by the door. He rested his elbows on his knees and stared at Lochinvar, watching as the little dragon poked its silver head into every cell. The creature was clever, that's for sure. And curious. As Driskoll watched, it climbed onto his knee, stretching its thin metal wings and chittering softly, "Skole. Skole?"

"Close," Driskoll said. "It's Driskoll."

"Dis-skole." The dragonet purred, the faint sound whirring in its long, sinuous neck.

Driskoll hummed softly, the tune to a traditional Promise song drifting into his memory. To his surprise, the creature tilted its mechanical head and began to purr more strongly, the sound shifting tone to match Driskoll's ballad.

"Driskoll," Kellach said impatiently. "stop that racket."

"But, Kellach, look! He's singing!"

Before Driskoll could protest further, Moyra let out a faint cry. "Uh-oh."

"Uh-oh-what?" Kellach looked back to see the iron door swing slightly open, Moyra frozen in front of it with her face in a grimace.

She cursed softly, looking back toward at the stairwell. "I . . . I think I set off a trap."

CHAPTER

11

"A trap?" Kellach looked concerned and confused. "But it didn't explode."

"Not all traps explode." Moyra scrambled up and scooped her tools back into the oilcloth. "I don't know what this one did, but whatever just happened, it can't be good. Quick, let's check out the room on the other side and get out of here." She tossed her red hair and shoved the door open. No use being cautious now.

Driskoll pushed himself to his feet, lifting the dragonet around the middle in order to carry the little creature. With an aggravated squawk, Lochinvar spread his wings and pushed off from Driskoll's hand.

The mechanical creature's wings flapped softly, guiding its erratic glide until it could grip Kellach's robes with all four feet, hanging nearly upside down with a surprised look stamped upon the silver features.

"Hey, good job, Locky," Kellach lifted the dragon to his shoulder. "I didn't know you could fly!"

"I don't think he knew either." Driskoll tagged along behind his brother, following Kellach and Moyra into the room behind the iron door.

"Wow," Moyra breathed.

The interior of the cell wasn't a cell at all. A small bed, complete with soft mattress and colored linens, stood in the far corner of the room. Near the door was a table, a washbasin, and a hand mirror intricately crafted from porcelain and silver. A tray stood by the washbasin, holding the remnants of two small cinnamon buns. Although the room had once been a prison, someone had gone to great length to make it at least passingly comfortable—a strange change from the flat stone walls outside.

"This makes no sense." Kellach patted the bed, testing the mattress with a firm touch. "Who would make a cell so comfortable?"

"This door is really thick." Moyra felt its steel timbre, testing the swing of the hinges. "Seals tight against the wall too. But my dad kept talking about 'hearing things' as if he'd overheard something he shouldn't. If it came from this cell, then the door was open."

"Or else," Kellach said, "it happened outside the door. Like someone refusing to enter the cell, maybe?"

"This cell's nicer than my bedroom," Driskoll shrugged. "I can't imagine who would fight to stay out. Especially if they'd seen the other options along the hallway."

"Maybe they weren't fighting to stay out of the room but to stay away from whoever was in here." Kellach shoved the bed, pushing it away from the wall in order to look behind it. As he did so, something fell to the ground with a soft thumping sound.

"Hey. Something was hidden back here." Kellach knelt,

reaching under the bed to retrieve a small book. He opened the book as he rose, staring at its pages quizzically. "It's written in a language I've never seen before."

Driskoll lifted the washbasin, looking inside curiously. "Clean. No water."

At the table near the door, Moyra lifted the mirror and then frowned. "It's broken," she said. "Whoever left this room either did it in a hurry or didn't want to go." She looked down at the floor by her feet, noting thin shards of glass under the table.

She knelt to look at the glass. "Kellach, look! Velvet fabric." She drew a scrap of fabric from under the table.

The scrap was dark, a blackish purple that shone like ink in the lantern light. Embroidered on what must have been the hem were strange golden characters. "They look like the ones in the book," Kellach said grimly.

"That cloth looks exactly like the robe that Zendric's friend was wearing." Driskoll said. "Hey! I get it. That woman, who-ever she is, was imprisoned here. She escaped from prison, found Zendric, and blackmailed him. Maybe Zendric even helped her escape." Driskoll gulped. "This is bad."

"Hmm," Kellach muttered. "I don't know. Something doesn't add up. Why is this cell so different from all the others? And what does Breddo have to do with all of it? There must be another clue in here."

Kellach searched the rest of the room. Lochinvar followed him, lunging from the bed into the air and humming Driskoll's ballad as he tried clumsily to fly. Still uncertain in the air, Lochinvar landed on the table with a staggering, swooped land-ing. The little dragon wove behind the washbasin, clicking and whirring as he furled his wings. Reaching the tray, Lochinvar cocked his head and began to sniff at the leftover pastry.

"Hey, cinnamon buns!" Driskoll said cheerily, spotting the small silver tray beside the washbasin. He walked over to it, reaching for one of them, when suddenly Lochinvar started hissing and lashing his tail.

All three kids turned and stared as Lochinvar's wings beat the air above the tray. The little dragonet bared silver fangs, a flicking tongue warning Driskoll away.

"What's wrong with him?" Driskoll jerked his hand back.

"Kellach, control that . . . that thing!"

Yet even as Moyra hissed the words, all three of them heard booted footsteps coming down the spiral stairwell.

"I told you, I heard a ringing! An alarm definitely went off." Gult's voice preceded him, and Kellach winced.

"But we don't have alarms," a second voice whined. "Do . . . Do we?"

"I dunno. I didn't think so. But I heard something start ringing. I definitely did." A pause, then Gult yelled, "I think I heard voices. I knew it! There's someone down here!"

"Prisoners escaping again," the second voice seemed slow and ponderous, as though the speaker had to force the words out. "We're not going to let them get away this time. This time we . . . we . . ."

" . . . kill 'em." Gult's sadistic laughter echoed his tromping footsteps. "Yeah. Danger to society. Gotta be . . . gotta be . . . like rabid dogs."

"What do we do now?" Driskoll whispered. "They're almost at the bottom of the stairs!"

"Drop your lantern. No, no, Driskoll! Open it!" Moyra flung the door of Driskoll's lantern open, bathing the room with bright light.

"Now, quickly!" Moyra grabbed Driskoll's sleeve and pulled him into the hall, diving into one of the other cells as Kellach dodged to follow.

The three kids crouched down in a dark cell, putting out the other lanterns in the last seconds before the guards entered the lower corridor. Lochinvar spun into the air and hovered by the ceiling of the hallway.

"Kellach, can't you control Lochinvar?" Moyra hissed.

"Locky!" Kellach whispered, trying to get the dragon's attention as the creature came to rest on a small rocky ledge against the ceiling of the corridor. "Get in here! You're going to—"

"Too late." Driskoll groaned. His hand tightened on his sword.

Five men staggered down the passageway, swords bared. The everburning torches they carried cast strange shadows across the floor. They all seemed unfamiliar with their swords flailing about with them and tapping at the walls. All of them moved slowly, their bodies wobbling on unsteady legs. The final man limped slightly, his wooden leg slightly shorter than his natural one. He carried a sword, like the others, though it was the first time the trio had ever seen the old watcher armed.

"Guffy—" Driskoll started. "But this isn't right. They don't look well. Something's wrong with them."

Moyra hushed him with an urgent hiss.

Behind the guards, the tremendous hulk of muscle and flesh that was Gult lumbered past, filling the hallway. "A light," he thundered. "At the end of the hall. Go!" He shoved two of the guards forward toward the iron door at the end of the passage, herding the others with the side of his heavy bronze mace.

Kellach stole a glance out at the guards as they swept by the cell door. He noted their glassy stare, the weak wrists that held sharp swords. The guards pushed through the open iron door and flooded into the small chamber at the end of the hallway.

"Now!" Kellach leaped up and scrambled out the doorway. He turned the corner and stopped dead in his tracks.

A pale-haired watcher stood in the corridor, staring dumbly up at the hissing Lochinvar. His eyes barely seemed to comprehend what he saw.

"Wait, don't—" But it was too late. Moyra and Driskoll were already reeling out of the cell, running so fast they didn't have time to stop. They stumbled into Kellach, who tumbled forward into the watcher. They all fell to the floor in a mass of flailing arms.

Behind them, the five watchers spilled out of the cell at the end of the corridor. Gult stomped out and planted his feet on the solid stone.

The fallen watcher whimpered from his seat on the ground, "Hey . . . Gult . . . you were right. People! But look, they've got a dragon!" His voice was filled with glee, face lighting up beneath his sturdy, but tilted, helmet.

Kellach, Driskoll, and Moyra sprang to their feet.

Guffy tottered forward, his wooden leg clattering against the stone floor. The kids made out Guffy's face, but his kind blue eyes looked unfocused and strange.

"Strange children running around in the prison?" he asked

with a curious shake of his head. "Prisoners! They're prisoners. That's why they're in prison." Guffy nodded his head, stamping his crutch on the ground threateningly.

"Guffy . . . don't you recognize us?" Kellach said.

"Escaping prisoners!" Gult howled, "Stop them!"

"Can't he tell we're not prisoners?" Driskoll drew his sword from its scabbard.

"I don't think they care!" Moyra cried.

And indeed, the guards seemed intent on the attack, their swords bright in the light of the torches. Together, the trio darted toward the stairs, hoping to get up the stairwell before the guards could catch them.

But they weren't fast enough.

Gult raced ahead of them and leaped onto the stairs, swinging his mace fearsomely and blocking their escape.

Driskoll raised his sword.

"Come on, Driskoll!" Moyra shouted. "There's no time for heroics!"

The guards surged forward. Moyra kicked out with her foot as one guard ran close, tripping him violently before he could grab her. She twisted like a cat, ducking out of the way as he fell to the floor in a heap.

His helmet rolled off his head, revealing a bright shock of red hair cropped into a thick bowl on top of his skull. The fallen guard reached for her again, arms waving in the air like noodles, but Moyra dodged aside.

"They're slow," she called to her friends. "All we have to do is avoid them!"

Another guard grabbed her by the arm, his weapon swishing

down with a killing strike. Moyra grabbed the fallen guard's helmet, raising it above her head desperately to block the blow.

The sword clanged against her hastily raised shield, ringing loudly and jarring Moyra's arms.

Kellach reached out and grabbed the guard's hand. *"Averiscus claritos!"* he yelled, and a massive electrical shock rushed down Kellach's arm. Blue sparks flew, and a brilliant flash of light, accompanied by the smell of burning hair, exploded within the corridor.

Driskoll stole the chance to shove another of the guards backwards, and the man reeled, woozy and confused from the blow.

"It's like they're drunk!" Driskoll shoved again, placing his sword against the guard's breastplate. He pushed the guard backwards into one of the cells. Driskoll grabbed the cell door and jerked it forward, hearing a solid click as it locked. "Ha!"

"Not drunk," Kellach said soberly, preparing another spell. "Drugged. The wyrmserum. It's got Gult and Guffy and these men too."

There were still three guards in the corridor behind him, their swords flashing and their eyes dazed and uncertain.

"Prisoners!" Gult howled, storming down the last few stairs and plunging into the fray. "Prisoners can't be released without papers!" His mace came down over Moyra, Gult's face flushed red with sadistic glee.

"Moyra!" Driskoll leaped forward.

Moyra swung her lantern fiercely, and it connected with Gult's mace. Sparks flew from the shattered metal lamp, the lantern crushing easily under the force of the impact.

Driskoll and Moyra each grabbed one of Gult's arms, hurling

85

themselves at the man. Their weight, along with his own ungainly movements, threw the huge man off balance.

Screaming bloody murder, Gult fell over.

"Run!" Kellach yelled, leaping over Gult and grabbing Moyra's hand. Moyra and Driskoll scrabbled to their feet, and together they raced up the stairway.

Footsteps charged along the corridor behind them. Gult's shouts carried through the echoing halls.

"Stop them!"

Driskoll glanced over his shoulder and saw three guards in close pursuit, their swords out and eyes wild.

"They're getting closer!" he gasped, running desperately to catch up. Moyra and Kellach squeezed back into the tunnel, past the open grate.

"Driskoll!" Moyra shouted. "Come on!"

Driskoll redoubled his speed and sheathed his sword in an instant.

He hurled himself at the grate, pulling with his arms and trying to wriggle into the narrow tunnel.

"Hold this!" Kellach threw his lantern to Moyra. As Moyra struggled to relight the lantern, Kellach gripped Driskoll's wrists, trying to pull his brother through before the guards arrived.

Driskoll felt hands clutching at his legs. Strong and powerful, they dragged him back.

"Guffy!" Driskoll recognized one of the guards behind him. The elderly, one-legged watcher moved slowly, lifting his sword even as the other watchers tried to drag Driskoll back into the hall. "Guffy, no!"

At the far end of the corridor, Gult strode like a giant, waving his mace and screaming, "Kill him, Guffy! Kill him before he escapes!"

To Driskoll's shock, Guffy seemed entirely content to carry out that order, raising his sword with a glazed, half-comprehending murmur of assent.

Driskoll shrieked, kicking wildly but unable to dislodge the two guards who were trying to drag him fully into the corridor.

"Kellach! Pull harder!"

As Kellach pulled Driskoll into the tunnel, he noticed Lochinvar swooping out into the passageway. The dragonet began huffing and puffing, churning up the bellows in his mechanical chest.

Guffy's sword began to drive forward to skewer Driskoll.

Just then, a roar and a burst of flames swept across the tunnel. Swooping down from above, Lochinvar was a shining silver tornado of wings and claws, his small mouth opening to release a miniature gout of flame.

The guards holding Driskoll were caught directly in the path of the fire. Their arms and tunics caught fire. They released Driskoll's legs.

Lochinvar landed on Guffy's arm. His silver claws dug and tore at the old man's flesh. Guffy screamed in pain.

With the guards no longer holding Driskoll's legs, Kellach managed to heft his brother into the small passage behind the grate. "Go, go!" He pushed Driskoll down the corridor. Moyra had already begun scooting down the tunnel, the lantern swinging wildly as she shouted for them to follow.

"Come on!" Moyra hissed. "The watchers can't get through here. It's too small. Once we get above ground, we can hide at my house."

87

"Good idea," Driskoll said, wiping soot and sparks from his pants. "But we'd better hurry, before those guards get loopy enough to follow us in here and get stuck."

"I'd love to see Gult stuck in these passages. It'd be just what he deserves," Kellach said smugly. Despite themselves, the three started giggling. They didn't stop until they reached Moyra's house.

CHAPTER

12

The tiny house in Broken Town was warm and friendly with a cozy fire heating the fireplace and lighting the main room.

Kellach pulled the curtains closed over the windows, shutting out the afternoon light.

"We have to be careful. The watch is probably looking for us by now."

On the mantel, Lochinvar spread his tinfoil wings to catch the updraft of heat from the fire. Driskoll scrubbed at his new belt and scabbard, trying to get some of the dirt from the tunnel off the new leather.

"If they even remember who we are," Driskoll scoffed. "They were all so drugged on that wyrmsoda."

"Wyrmserum," Kellach corrected.

"Yeah, wyrmserum," Driskoll shook his head. "All those guards were poisoned. Even Guffy!"

"I know. If only we could figure out how they're administering the poison, we might be able to stop it."

Moyra came out of the back room. "My dad's in bed. He's still sleeping."

Kellach sat down in a rickety chair beside his brother, placing his feet on the hearthstone near the fire. He drew the small journal out of his pocket and gazed at it for a moment.

"Is that the book you found behind the bed?" Driskoll asked.

"Yeah. But it's all in some strange language." Kellach opened it once more, flipping slowly through the pages of the journal. Each leaf of paper was covered with unusual scrawling. There were symbols that made no sense even to the young wizard's trained eye. "I'm not even sure these are letters. They look like pictures, but weird ones. Maybe each picture is a word? Or part of a word?" Kellach began muttering to himself, slowly turning the pages as he studied the book.

"Is there any way to translate it?" Moyra asked, glancing down at the incomprehensible symbols.

"Well, usually I'd take it to Zendric." Kellach sighed.

"Well, that's not really an option right now," she snapped.

Kellach frowned.

"I'm sorry, Kellach," Moyra continued. "But there's a very good chance that Zendric's involved in this. The woman at his house, and the fact that he was at the prison before all this started happening. We can't risk it."

Kellach glared at the journal, not wanting to meet Moyra's eyes. "Fine. Just let me concentrate." He ran his thumb across the edges of the journal's yellowy pages, flicking through them idly while his mind focused on the problem.

"These symbols," Kellach pointed at the book. Locky flew

over to Kellach's shoulder with a fussy sniff. "I've seen them before—or something like them."

"Kell-ack." Lochinvar climbed down the wizard's arm, stuffing his shiny, silver muzzle into the book. "Make words?"

"Locky, *ow*!" Kellach tried to pull the little dragon from his arm, wincing as the creature's claws pinched against his bare skin. The dragonet continued to poke at the journal, scrabbling fiercely. Eventually, Kellach got the little creature to sit on the arm of the chair. Lochinvar continued to stare eagerly at the pages of the journal.

"Ugh," Kellach suddenly reached up and pinched the bridge of his nose. "I just got a terrible headache."

"I'll get you a glass of water. I'm afraid we don't have much else." Moyra moved from the fire, heading toward the small kitchen area of the little house.

"No, hang on—" Kellach closed his eyes. Suddenly, a look of amazement spread across his features. "Gods! I can see!"

"What? With your eyes closed?" Driskoll laughed.

"Yes!" Kellach opened his eyes again, winced, and closed them. "But when I open my eyes, the headache gets worse."

"What are you seeing?"

"I can see . . . I can see my hand. And the arm of the chair. And you . . . you look really strange, Driskoll. Like you're ten times bigger, and sort of curved."

"How many fingers am I holding up?" Driskoll lifted his hand.

"Three."

Moyra and Driskoll exchanged surprised glances. "You're right." Driskoll and ran his fingers through his hair. "How are you doing that?"

On the arm of the rickety chair, Lochinvar chirped happily and began to flap his wings. "I can see through his eyes."

Kellach opened his own and stared down at the little clockwork dragon.

"One heck of a machine," Moyra looked concerned. "Especially if he's in your mind. That's just not safe, Kellach. Who knows what that creature is looking for?"

Kellach closed his eyes again and stared through the eyes of his new pet. "It isn't like that, Moyra. It's like looking through a window. Or one of those fun-house mirrors."

Lochinvar twisted his head around, and Kellach found himself staring at the journal that lay, forgotten, on his lap. He let out a sudden shout as he caught sight of its yellowed pages.

"Hey! I can read it!"

Kellach laughed out loud, opening his eyes and grinning. "I guess Locky knows the language. And if he does, then I do, when I look through his eyes."

"Oh, Kellach, I don't like that. This little creature can read the language of that woman? That's dangerous!" Moyra stood up, pacing the room and shooting an evil glance at the silver dragon. "She made that thing, I guess. It came with her, in any case. And it reads her language, so that proves it. It might be working with her. A spy, telling her everything we're doing."

"Come on, Moyra," Driskoll fidgeted, seeing the hurt look in his brother's eyes. "You can't believe that."

"I very well do, and you should too!" She shook her head, red hair like fire, as her voice took on the shade of worry. "If it's a spy, then nothing we find out is safe. It'll report to her and tell her everything."

"And how can he do that, exactly?" Kellach said, his eyes narrowing. "Locky can hardly fly, and he's got no more idea where that woman is than we do. It'd be like searching for a needle in a haystack."

"Well . . . he could . . ." Moyra stumbled for a good reply.

Kellach continued, "Lochinvar's got no more idea what's going on here than we do. If he can help me read this language, then that's getting somewhere. And we need every clue we can find. If you can read it instead—" Kellach held out the book to Moyra. "Then be my guest."

Moyra stared at the book sullenly. "You know I can't."

"Right, then." Kellach turned the journal back around and opened it once more, showing it to the dragon. Locky chirruped with mild interest. "C'mon, Locky. Take a look."

Kellach closed his eyes once more as Lochinvar stood up on the arm of the chair and pushed his muzzle into the journal pages with a little cheep.

The dragonet seemed almost to be reading to himself, bobbing his head up and down as Kellach flipped each page and uttered small, incomprehensible burbles and meeps.

"What does it say?" Even Moyra couldn't hide her interest, looking over Kellach's shoulder at the squiggles on the page.

"It's still fuzzy. Sort of like a code, but—" The apprentice wizard closed his eyes and flipped through the pages eagerly, reading a snippet here and there.

"Read it, read it!" Driskoll sat up, poking his brother's shins with eagerness.

"It's a diary. Most of the entries are just what she ate, what she wore—simple things. It looks like scribbles, like someone was writing very fast or trying to hide what they were writing in this book."

Driskoll stared quizzically. "Does it say who wrote it?"

"Nope." Kellach flipped the page and took in a breath. "Hold on. This one's different."

"What?" Driskoll said. "What does it say?"

"I can't believe it. It's the recipe for wyrmserum. 'Wyrmserum is used for numbing the mind and controlling someone's will. Best brewed when the moon is full, with aconite, bunyip horn, or unicorn hoof—' "

"Unicorn hoof?" Moyra cocked her head. "Do they really use that?

"It's the name of an herb. It just looks like a unicorn's hoof. It grows in the shadows of churches." Kellach continued to read, turning the page as Lochinvar burbled and nuzzled the hand that held the pages. "This part of the book seems to be a notebook, like for school, where someone was writing down the things they learned."

Driskoll poked at the little journal. "Does that book say anything about the antidote for wyrmserum?"

Kellach flipped the pages back and forth. "I don't see one. But, gods!" Kellach opened his eyes and stared at the little dragon for a moment before going back to the text. "Some of the ingredients in this wyrmserum recipe are very rare. Extremely valuable, and almost impossible to find."

Driskoll said, "Didn't Arren say that someone was stealing alchemy supplies from his warehouse?"

Kellach nodded. "That's not the worst bit. One of these ingredients is more than just rare. It's incredibly dangerous. Medusa venom."

94

"That's one of those herb code names, right? Like unicorn hoof?"

Kellach opened his eyes and shook his head grimly. "Nope. That's the real thing. And it has to be fresh. The only way to get it is from a medusa herself."

"Medusa?" Moyra asked.

"You know, a snake-haired woman?" Driskoll prompted. "If one looks you in the eye, you'll turn to stone."

"Good to see you remember some of the ancient legends as well as those new love ballads you keep singing lately," Kellach teased.

Driskoll smiled, eager to relate what he knew. "There's a myth that the original medusa was cursed by a powerful sorcerer because she spurned his love. What's more accurately known about them is that they're an evil race living on an island, far over the mountains to the south. Humans don't go there. They're cannibalistic and they dine on their enemies."

"*Ew.*" Moyra wrinkled her nose. "That's disgusting."

Driskoll continued, "They're evil to the core, and worse, they're not like trolls or orcs. Medusas are smart." Driskoll turned to Kellach, "Could the woman that Zendric's been seeing, the woman in the hood, could she be a medusa?"

Kellach nodded. "That's what I was thinking. She always wears that hood as if she doesn't want anyone to see her face."

"Because if she looks anyone in the eye, they'll be turned to stone." Moyra shivered.

"Stone! That's it." Kellach shut the journal and jumped out of his chair. "I just remembered where I saw these symbols." Kellach grinned. "The statue in Main Square. The one that Pralthamus was dedicating yesterday."

Driskoll nodded suddenly, his mind racing. "That's right! It had all kinds of weird squiggles along the hem of the robe and on the base. But . . . what if a medusa made that statue?"

Kellach's face was grim. "I think that's exactly who made that statue. In fact, I think that statue isn't a statue at all."

"What?" yelped Moyra. "You mean that's not a statue of Elisa in Main Square. It *is* Elisa in Main Square?" Moyra stared, realizing the horror of that statement.

Driskoll shuddered. "Right." He remembered the cool, calm visage of the marble woman in the square, and the eerie resemblance she bore to the lost watcher. "A medusa. She's behind all of this. The statue, the wyrmserum. It all makes sense."

"Let's go to Main Square," Kellach said, helping Lochinvar back up onto his shoulder. "I want to get another look at that statue. Now that we have Locky, we'll be able to read the writing on the stone. And if we're lucky, we'll finally be on our way to solving this mystery."

"And if we're not lucky, we'll get turned to stone ourselves." Driskoll's face screwed up in worry.

"Don't be such a scaredy-cat, Driskoll." Kellach laughed, shaking his little brother by the shoulder. "After all, what could possibly go wrong?"

CHAPTER

13

People filled Curston's Main Square, the evening air ringing with the celebration of the second day of the Promise Festival. Much like the day before, the market was open until an hour after curfew. Folks crowded the stands buying wine and sweetbreads as well as trinkets and prizes before they had to hurry home.

Watchers stood on every corner, overseeing the unusual evening festivities. As Driskoll passed one watcher, he stared up into the man's glazed eyes. The watcher yawned and muttered to himself, paying no attention to the people in the plaza.

"I think all the watchers here are poisoned too—"

Kellach gripped his arm before he could finish. "Look!"

Driskoll looked at where his sharp-eyed brother was pointing. He saw a knot of watchers pushing their way through the crowd. Torin's loud voice demanded passage, scattering the revelers before them.

"Quick." Kellach shoved Driskoll and Moyra down under the wagon of a sword salesman, diving beneath the wide axel that spread between the wagon wheels. "Hide!"

Torin and his small group of watchers passed within only a few feet of the three kids, laughing uproariously. Driskoll saw that his father's eyes were bloodshot and his face was pale and drawn despite the vigor of his laughter.

"Pay up!" Torin yelled, shoving the sword merchant. "Pralthamus has imposed taxes on all inhabitants of the city to pay for the festival!"

"What?" the merchant protested.

"You heard me." Torin laughed. "If you can't pay me in copper, we'll take it in goods! Go ahead, boys."

The merchant stared in shock as the watchers ripped through his stock of swords. "How can you do this? You're running honest business out of town."

Torin picked him up by the arms and shook him, shouting, "Don't give me any lip now, or you'll answer to the wizard!"

The watchers crowed around as Torin shook the helpless little man, wobbling him back and forth until a pouch fell from the man's waistcoat. "There's our taxes, boys!" The other watchers laughed, their voices thick and toneless. One bent down to scoop up the small money pouch, and Driskoll caught a glimpse of his red-rimmed, glassy eyes.

"Wizard?" hissed Moyra. "He must mean Zendric."

"*Ssh!*" was Kellach's only reply.

"I can't believe that's Dad," Driskoll said, aghast. "First he was acting like a three-year-old, now he's a complete bully."

"It's not him. It's the wyrmserum." Grimly, Kellach watched their father and his men weaving a strange, torpid line through Curston's great marketplace.

"Do you think Pralthamus really imposed another tax?" whispered Moyra.

"If he's under the same spell, I bet he did." Driskoll said.

Kellach nodded. "It's spreading. By tomorrow, I bet every official in the city will be under the spell of the wyrmserum. We've got to hurry."

"There's the statue," Moyra wasn't listening anymore. Her attention was completely focused on the stone figure near the center of the square. "Hurry, Kellach, we've got to get out of here before they see us."

"All right, Locky, you know what to do. Quickly, while everyone's watching Torin and the watchers." Lifting his arm, Kellach thrust the mechanical dragon into the air. Lochinvar flitted upward and then settled on top of the statue.

Lochinvar fluttered behind the wide stone hood of the statue, clutching its marble shoulder with his silvery claws. He tried to hide behind the statue's ornate marble ripples as much as possible, ducking beneath the stone woman's arm and clawing his way down to the hem of her robe.

Kellach grinned and pulled out the journal and a pencil from a pocket of his apprentice robes. He turned to a blank page then closed his eyes, whispering to himself as he directed the little dragon to read the strange markings.

"Got it," Kellach opened his eyes triumphantly, waving the journal page in his brother's face. "It's some kind of a riddle. Here, listen."

Straightening the paper upon the ground, Kellach read quietly.

I send a plea that you might seek
a serpent's secret nest.
Where north is north
The needle spins
And east becomes

"And east becomes what? " Driskoll asked.

"I don't know." Kellach said, looking more closely at his notes. "That's all it says."

Lochinvar fluttered back and hopped onto Kellach's arm. Kellach rubbed the dragonet's head, murmuring praise while the dragon's violet eyes spun.

"I don't get it," Driskoll took the journal from his brother's hand and scanned the writing. "This doesn't make any sense."

Kellach looked up. "Well, it is a riddle. Whoever made this statue deliberately put these runes on them. The riddle is a message to someone."

"Who?"

"Other medusas?" Moyra suggested.

"How do you get that?"

" 'Serpent's secret nest,' " Moyra repeated. "That must mean a medusa's hideaway, right? Maybe Zendric's visitor wrote the riddle on the statue like some kind of direction. She wants to lead other medusas to her secret haven. To where she's hiding."

The thought made Driskoll wince. "So there could be more than one of them in town?"

"It's possible. Say the medusa wants control of Curston. She uses the wyrmserum to put all the city officials under mind control and blackmails Zendric to help her. Meanwhile her friends show up to help her take over the town. She has to find some way to tell them where to find her."

Kellach shook his head, holding Locky so tight that the little dragon whimpered. "Maybe. But there has to be more to the message. The last line is clearly missing something. This must be only the beginning."

"So, where's the rest of it?"

"There must be another statue with the rest of the riddle carved into it."

"The warehouse." Driskoll's eyes went wide. "Remember the crate you dropped on the bandit? It had a statue in it."

Moyra nodded, tapping her fingers against her chin as she considered it.

"Wait a second," Moyra said. "If we find the other statue, and it tells us how to find the medusa's hideaway, then what?"

"We find her and we stop her," Kellach said. "Somehow."

"Maybe we should get some help? Last time we tried something like this . . . "

Kellach shook his head. "Who's going to help us? Dad, Pralthamus, the watch—they're all under her spell."

"And we can't trust Zendric," Driskoll added.

Kellach glared at him.

"Well, we can't!" Driskoll said. "Didn't you hear? Dad just said that a wizard was involved, that he was telling him and Pralthamus what to do. I know you don't want to listen to anything bad about Zendric, but it's looking more and more like Zendric's behind all this. "

Kellach crossed his arms. "It doesn't matter. We don't need Zendric. We're Knights of the Silver Dragon, remember? It's our duty to defend this city, and we can do it without him."

"He's right, Moyra," Driskoll nodded. "We've got to help the town before it's too late."

Moyra threw up her hands. "Fine. Let's go."

As they ran out of Main Square, Kellach never noticed that Lochinvar remained behind, his head cocked as if listening to a half-heard sound.

Chirping, Lochinvar took to the sky. Rather than follow Kellach, Driskoll, and Moyra, Lochinvar set out on another course. Down a long, dark alley, Lochinvar sailed. He landed with great care upon the outstretched hand of a woman in a velvet cloak.

She reached into a pocket of her cloak and withdrew a small oak wand, sliding it into an aperture between the gears. It clicked into place and began to glow with a faint amethyst light that matched the shine of the dragonet's eyes.

"Now, my little fellow," the woman breathed, her velvet robes rustling. "Exactly what have you been up to?"

CHAPTER

14

"Driskoll! Catch!"

Moyra threw down the rope from atop the warehouse windowsill. After scaling the side of the building, she had tied a strand of rope around a hook above the broken window. Now she stood on the ledge outside the window, waiting for her friends to meet her at the top.

"You sure you want to do this?" Moyra called down for the third time. Driskoll grabbed hold of the rope and tugged on it, signaling that he was ready to climb.

"I'm sure." Driskoll said.

"I could go in there and get what we needed. I'd be back in a flash."

"No, Moyra," Kellach called up. "It's too dangerous for any of us to go in alone."

Moyra looked grumpy, no doubt imagining the heavy tread of Driskoll's boots and the sound of Kellach bumping into crates in the dark.

"Don't say I didn't warn you," she called.

The ancient wall creaked and echoed as Driskoll scaled the side of the building. Gripping the edge of the windowsill, Driskoll called down to his brother, "Your turn, Kellach!"

"Wait," Kellach looked back over his shoulders. "I still haven't found Locky. Where could he have gone?"

"Good riddance," Moyra muttered. "I don't want him spying on us and telling the medusa where to find us."

"But without Locky, I won't be able to read the runes on the statue," Kellach said.

"You could copy down the symbols," Driskoll suggested. "Then you can read them when Locky comes back. Come on. We'd better hurry before someone hears us!"

Kellach hung his head, defeated, and gripped the rope. After he had made it to the top, the trio stepped together through the broken windowpane.

"I'm glad Arren didn't have the time to fix this window," Moyra whispered.

Beneath them, tall stack of cedar crates provided easy access to the warehouse floor.

As Driskoll and Kellach made their way gingerly down to the ground, Moyra replaced the boards that had covered the broken window and tiptoed down the pile of crates. Her feet crunched softly as she landed on the straw that covered the earthen floor.

Kellach looked up toward the ceiling, goose bumps covering his skin. The last time he had been in this warehouse, he had almost been killed. He looked at his brother and knew he was thinking the same thing.

Driskoll ducked his head sheepishly. His hand felt for the hilt of his sword, reassuring himself that it was still there.

"Planning to use that?" Kellach eyed his brother.

"If I need to," Driskoll said boldly. The words came out louder than he had intended, and Moyra hissed at him to be silent.

The trio rushed through the warehouse to the spot where the boys had last seen the statue's shattered crate. The ground was covered with packing straw and broken bits of wood. But the statue was nowhere to be found.

Kellach crouched down and picked up one of the pieces of wood, examining it closely.

"This is where the crate was," Driskoll said, "But where's the statue?"

"It looks like Arren's taken it away," Moyra said.

"Great." Driskoll threw his hands up. "What are we doing to do now?"

Kellach stood up and brushed away the straw that clung to his robes. "We're going to have a look at the statue."

"*Um,* Kellach," Driskoll said, "in case you hadn't noticed, the statue is gone."

"I know. That's because it's in Arren's office." Kellach marched ahead.

"How do you know that?" Driskoll asked.

"Just look." Kellach pointed down. A trail cut through the layer of clean straw on the hard-packed dirt floor. "The statue was obviously dragged across the warehouse floor," Kellach explained as they followed the trail, "then carried up these stairs." Straw littered a wooden stairway that led up to a balcony. At the far end of the balcony, they could just make out the outline of a door.

"Of course!" Moyra said.

"So that doorway up there, that's Arren's office?" Driskoll said.

"I think so. Moyra, you'd better go first."

Moyra placed one hand on the banister and her other hand on the warehouse wall, tentatively checking each stair before placing her weight on it.

"Do you think it's trapped?" Driskoll piped up.

"Arren said he'd had a lot of break-ins," Kellach said. "He's probably taken extra precautions with his personal possessions."

The three moved up the staircase cautiously, the boys following Moyra as she checked each stair for traps. As they reached the top of the stairs, the balcony came into view. An intricately carved railing lined the edge of the balcony. At the far end of the ledge sat the door to Arren's office.

Moyra tentatively stepped up onto the balcony, then she motioned for them to stop.

"What?" Driskoll and Kellach chorused, earning them a hard stare from Moyra.

"There's a large metal pressure plate here. It's been hidden beneath the wooden planks of the balcony. Look, you can see the edges of it."

Indeed, the faint edges of metal shone with a strange luster against the hard oak, faintly revealing itself despite the paint that covered both.

"I can't tell what it does." She frowned.

"Whatever it is, it can't be good," Driskoll said.

The plate stretched beneath the planks of the balcony for several feet, vanishing under the longer boards that held the balcony tightly against the wall. Moyra took a long look at the plate, the concealing board, and the area surrounding it.

"Nothing." Moyra shook her head. "I don't see anything that it connects to."

Driskoll and Kellach watched as she ran her fingers along the plate, seeking anything out of place.

She sighed. "There's no way to know how far this plate goes, or what will happen if we walk on it." She rolled up her tools and stuffed them back in her pack. "Better to avoid it entirely."

Kellach peered down at the plate, staring at it intently. "What are you going to do?"

Moyra removed her shoes and tied them by the leather laces to her belt. She stretched her toes and grinned. "Just watch."

Moyra climbed tentatively onto the railing that circled the outer edge of the balcony, careful to keep her weight off the floor beneath her. The banister was sturdy enough to carry her, but Moyra had to balance precariously.

Placing one foot securely before the other, Moyra began moving toward Arren's office door, balancing more than ten feet above the hard dirt floor. Moyra held her arms out to either side and barely wobbled as she walked.

"By St. Cuthbert!" Driskoll muttered. "That's so brave."

Moyra couldn't hear him, but Kellach could. He turned and stared at his younger brother.

Driskoll blushed to the roots of his hair. "Well, it is."

Just then, about halfway to the door at the end of the balcony, Moyra stopped.

"What is it?" Kellach called.

Feeling with her toe, Moyra tapped her foot against something hard and cool. She froze. Then she crouched down on the banister to see what she had discovered.

"It's a pipe." Moyra pointed at a small metal tube that crawled down the side of the railing and vanished under the balcony floor.

Moyra smiled soberly, her knees holding tight to the railing while her fingers explored the tube. "Actually, this is good. Now I know what this trap is. It's gas, or something that will come out of these tubes if someone steps on that plate. Look, there are other tubes in the banister."

Glancing around, she pointed them out, the metal openings buried in the intricate carvings of the railing.

She scooted back along the railing. Then she removed her shoes from her belt and tied the laces together at their longest points.

"Watch this." Moyra tossed her shoes onto the balcony floor, still holding the laces. She then dragged the shoes back toward her. Kellach and Driskoll stared, covering their noses and mouths and backing up to the edge of the stairwell.

In a moment, her shoes passed over a section of the hidden plate. A sharp puffing sound warned that the plate had been triggered. Three small tubes released their contents into the air, and a thin, watery liquid sprayed inward from the balcony railing. It covered the planks with sticky, clear liquid.

Clutching the banister between her legs and balancing away from the center of the balcony, Moyra was untouched by the stream. But her eyes watered at the immediate and severe stench that wafted toward her from the liquid.

"Alchemists," she muttered. "And they say we thieves work too much with poison."

Moyra tied her shoes once more, and hung them again from the belt at her waist.

"You two are going to have to stay back there," Moyra said.

"Are you kidding?" Driskoll said. "There might be something dangerous inside that room."

"I know," Moyra smiled back over her shoulder. "But you can't make it across that trap. I can handle it. I'll let you know what's inside Arren's office, and if it's too much for me, then we'll all make a run for it. Okay?"

Kellach nodded tersely.

Moyra began another trek, inch by inch, upon the railing. At last, Moyra found she was able to reach the far wall. She squatted again on the railing, clenching it between her legs, and pulled out her tools once more.

Arren's office door was made of thick, carved rosewood inlaid against oak planking. Moyra gauged it for strength and decided it was far too thick and sturdy for even a tough warrior to kick it down—Arren was serious about protecting this office.

Hoping to get a better look at the lock, she gently leaned one hand on the door. It pushed inward on rigid hinges, without a single creak.

The door was unlocked.

CHAPTER

15

I guess after that trap, there's no need for a lock!" Moyra laughed. She slipped from the banister directly into the room, her bare feet finding the unexpected softness of a plush rug just within the door.

"Wow," she murmured.

"What?" Kellach called, as the boys leaned forward on the stairs, peering into the room from the far edge of the balcony. They could just barely make out some of the details through the doorway.

The office looked about as large as a bedroom. They could see the floor was covered by a knotwork carpet, soft and brightly colored. Along the back wall, mahogany and rosewood cabinets cast shadows beneath darkly colored windowpanes. Arren's desk stood like a predator in the center of the room directly in front of the door. It hunched over legs ended in lion paws that were square and thick and clawed.

"Can you see this? This place is amazing." Then, suddenly Moyra yelped and leaped back.

"What?" Driskoll started forward onto the balcony, his hand on his sword. Kellach grabbed his brother's wrist as they heard Moyra's voice once more.

"Um, I think I found the statue." Moyra gulped. "It startled me, standing there in the shadows. It looks like a young watcher shuffling cards. Is this the one from the crate?"

"That's it!" Kellach craned forward to try to get a view of the statue. "Does it have carvings on it? Can you see them?"

"*Uh...*" Moyra crouched down. "Yup, I see them. Along the base. And there are some on the cards."

"Can you copy the symbols onto a piece of paper?" Kellach asked hopefully.

"Hold on." There was a sound of scuffling, and Driskoll almost hopped up and down in excitement. When Moyra appeared at the door, she waved a page covered in scribblings. "Got it."

"Excellent!" Kellach paused. "Wait! Before you go, are there any books?"

Moyra sighed in exasperation. "This is no time for reading, Kellach! We've got to get out of here before someone catches us."

"No, I'm serious. This is important. Arren's an alchemist, remember? He might have a book in there about wyrmserum that could tell us how to make an antidote."

"Oh, all right." Moyra began to poke about the room, and Kellach and Driskoll could hear her opening and closing drawers and cabinet doors.

"Aha!" she said in triumph. "Found it! Arren's got a whole cabinet full of books. There are a zillion of them."

"Read us the titles, Moyra." Kellach said.

She hunched down before the cabinet, drawing out first one book and then another.

"All right, Kellach," Moyra murmured. "Let me know if any of these sound right to you."

"*Gadgets of the Gnomes, Vicious Herbs: How to Care for Them, Who to Feed Them,*" Moyra intoned. "I've got *Flora of the Deep Fell; Potions and Proxies;* and a book entirely on the uses of a dragon's corpse, from the top of its head to the tip of the tail." Moyra scoffed, "As if anyone could ever kill one of those mighty beasts." Then, near the bottom of the pile, she pulled out a slim volume bound in green leather. She glanced at the title. "Kellach! This one's called *Venoms, Rare and Mysterious: Serpents, Snakes, Dragons, and Medusas.*"

"That'll do!" Kellach said, as he and Driskoll exchanged victorious grins. "Bring it out here."

Moyra climbed back up on the railing, carrying the book under one arm and the paper under the other. She closed the office door with one foot and shimmied down the banister, hopping down beside the boys.

"Here is your riddle!" Moyra waved the paper triumphantly. "And here's your book." She passed the green book to Kellach.

The trio sat down on the top stair. Kellach opened the book cautiously, staring at the fancy script written on ash-colored pages. Drawings filled each page, elaborate pictures of snakes of all kinds: short and thick, coiled, and giant. On one page, the writing flowed out of a pair of fangs, like venom dripped upon the page.

"Medusas," Moyra read slowly, recognizing a particularly terrifying sketch of a woman. The woman's back was turned to the artist, and her hair—a thousand little snakes—twisted like vipers down her curved spine.

"There it is," Driskoll pointed. "Wyrmserum."

Kellach read quietly. "It controls the mind—yes, yes, we knew that—also has side effects of hallucinations, paranoia, dreamlessness. That's interesting. It must be what Breddo is dealing with." He shook his head restlessly.

Kellach turned the page and took in a sharp breath.

"Listen to this: wyrmserum is best when given with bread, or inside cooked goods, as the yeast covers both the scent and taste of the wyrmserum itself." Kellach looked up. "I think I know how the serum is being administered," he said slowly.

"How?" Driskoll asked.

"Cinnamon buns."

"You're right, Kellach," Driskoll said. "In the cell where Moyra's dad was kept, as well as in the cell at the end of the corridor, there were cinnamon buns."

"And Dad was eating one at the festival, and so were Gult, Guffy, and the others at Watchers' Hall. The buns were given to the watchers by a merchant. That's what Guffy said when we went to get Breddo." Kellach steepled his fingers. "I think someone has put the drug into the buns. The watchers wouldn't question it. They always get cinnamon buns at the Promise Festival, as gifts for the year's labor."

Moyra shook her head. "But my dad had to be given the drugs before the festival. He was far more drugged than Torin was, as if he'd been under the effects longer. Torin just started acting strangely last night."

"True. Dad was fine yesterday morning." Driskoll eyes flickered down to his sword.

"So, first," Kellach pondered, "the drug has to be relatively fast acting. Torin was affected by it within about twelve hours. Breddo is worse, so I'd bet he was drugged, oh, maybe a day before that. About the time . . . hey, about the time whoever was in that iron cell would have been leaving the prison!"

"So, you think they drugged him to make sure he wouldn't remember what he saw through the bars of his cell?" Moyra asked.

"I'd bet that's it. What was it that Breddo was saying when we took him from the prison?"

Driskoll piped up, "Something about keeping his ear to the stone, and the stone speaking. And the cell at the end of the corridor."

Moyra stubbornly set her chin. "I bet that woman—that medusa—wasn't imprisoned in the cell. I bet she was using the cell as a place to make this drug. A place where she wouldn't be disturbed."

"You can say that again," Driskoll muttered to himself. "Nobody's going to disturb you down there!"

Ignoring him, Moyra continued, "My dad must have been some sort of a test case. She fed him the pastries to see what the drug would do. To make sure it would work."

"That would explain why he's having more severe effects," Kellach agreed.

Driskoll poked at the book. "So what about the antidote? Is there anything we can put together to wake them all up from this spell?"

Kellach turned the page, his face brightening. "Here it is!" he whispered eagerly. "It needs entwistle—that's a common herb—mother's root, echacia, yam, and black agate—powdered of course. Yew breath is a bit hard to find. But we can probably get it in one of the shops in the Wizard's Quarter." Kellach took in a breath. "Oh no."

"What?" Driskoll clambered to look closer.

Kellach slumped his shoulders and pointed at the book. "The last ingredient is medusa tears."

"They can't mean real medusa tears," Moyra said. "I can't imagine those evil beasts would ever cry."

"I'm afraid they do," Kellach said. "But I have no idea how we'll be able to get them—unless we can find the medusa and make her cry ourselves!"

Suddenly, a sharp noise outside in the warehouse put Moyra on the edge of her toes. She drew her dagger from its sheath in a smooth, silent motion. "Did you hear that?" she whispered.

It was a strange, buzzing, flapping noise that echoed among the eaves of the warehouse. The trio leaned over the edge of the stairwell and watched as the sound approached.

Silver sparkled beneath the stairs, and the sound of wings reached their ears at the same time as the dragonet's cry.

Lochinvar flitted in long strands of pale moonlight, his silver scales casting reflections that bounced against the office walls. Moyra muffled her cry of surprise.

"Locky!"

Kellach jumped to his feet. "There you are! We were looking all over for you. But how did you get in here?"

Lochinvar burbled. The sound of his voice echoed among the pillared crates in the warehouse. Kellach tried to grab him, "Locky, calm down. What are you trying to tell me?"

Kellach tried to keep his voice to a hushed whisper as he gripped the dragonet's muzzle and clamped it shut so that the dragonet could not continue his cries. The little mechanical beast broke away, landing on the banister. He shook his head and chirruped loudly.

"Make him be quiet, Kellach! He's making too much noise! It's going to bring the watch!" Moyra tucked the book and the piece of paper into her pocket, quickly preparing to leave.

With another chirrup, the little dragon lifted off the railing and flew out the nearest open window.

"Locky come back!" Kellach whispered. But the dragonet was gone.

A tremendous slam resounded like the tolling of an iron bell through the wooden structure. A long, drawn, sliding noise followed.

The kids' heads jerked down as one, staring in wide-eyed horror at the warehouse doors. A long swath of light punctuated the shadows of the warehouse. The entrance of the loading bay was open. They had been found.

16

One by one, the three kids slipped to the edge of the stairway, grasping the railing of the stairs and sliding between the bars.

Kellach went first, followed by Driskoll, then Moyra. She hung for a moment, hands clutching the railing and her feet dangling in darkness. Then, closing her eyes, she let go.

The ground slammed into her with a solid thump, knocking Moyra to her side on the straw floor. As she landed, her ankle twisted beneath her. She swallowed a cry of pain, pressing her face against the dirt. Driskoll's face dropped, and he and Kellach reached in tandem to help their friend to her feet.

"I heard something!" Though the voice was slow and dulled, it was unmistakably Gwinton, the watcher who had been so kind to Kellach and Driskoll only a night before. The sturdy dwarf's footsteps tromped through the warehouse, as he called to his men. "You two, *er,* three, take the right. Do something. And, *um.* You go right. I'll go the other way. What's that called again?" He giggled a moment. "Never mind. I'll go straight."

The watchers walked through the warehouse, their steps slow and confused. Quickly, the boys helped Moyra stumble to a tall crate, hiding themselves in its shadows.

Looking past the crates, Driskoll could see the watchers, glassy-eyed and strange in the night. "Oh no." he whispered.

There, in the light of the loading doors, a short, hawk-nosed gentleman with long, flowing pale robes strode into the warehouse, a look of fury on his beaky features. He directed the watchers in their search, climbing the stairs toward the balcony with a hurried, anxious step.

"Arren." Kellach frowned.

"If we can just make it outside the building before too many of the watch show up, then maybe we can slip away." Moyra winced.

Kellach peeked out behind the crate. They were only a few feet from the open doors. He saw Gwinton and his men giggling through the corridors of the warehouse. They called to one another in slow, dragging tones. Kellach hastily slipped back behind the crate.

Arren's voice shouted down from above. From the tone of his voice, they could tell he was furious, but they couldn't make out the words.

Kellach grimaced. He didn't particularly need to know what Arren was saying. It was clear that he'd just discovered the mess in his office. Now he would tear the warehouse apart until he found them.

Moyra glared at Kellach. "Your little dragon betrayed us. He told the watch where to find us."

"There's no time for that now, Moyra," Driskoll whispered.

"We might be able to make a run for it," Kellach said. "Put your arms around our shoulders." He and Driskoll lifted Moyra to her feet.

They peered out behind the crate again.

Only a few watchers stood in front of the doorway. Kellach recognized the obvious signs of wyrmserum in their faces. Their sullen stares had little intelligence.

To make it to the door, they would have to run in full view of the watchers.

"Can you do it?" Kellach asked Moyra, his gaze flickering down to her ankle. The girl's only response was a tight-lipped nod.

Two watchers crossed paths near the doors, waving cheerily at each other and pausing to giggle at the tall stacks of crates. When they turned away, Kellach moved.

"Now."

All three darted from the crates, sprinting toward the exit as fast as they could go.

Fifteen steps away, the open doors split the dark wall with a ray of light. Ten steps, and they could see the alley just outside. Two steps. The doors were wide and bright, and the torchlit alleyway was a paradise compared to the stifling darkness of the warehouse.

Then a great shout went up behind them. Kellach risked a glance over his shoulder. He saw Arren standing on his balcony, hand outstretched, pointing at them.

"Thieves!" Arren screamed. "Those children are thieves! Call the watch!"

They ran out the door and turned the corner. But, instead of a clear alleyway and freedom, they saw another group of watchers. These watchers had their swords in hand and were headed right for them.

The group was led by Torin.

"The watch!" Moyra panted. "They're right in front of us!"

"And behind us too!" Kellach thumbed back at Arren, Gwinton, and the others, who were exiting the warehouse in their wake. "What do we do?"

"I can't run far—my ankle." Moyra winced.

Driskoll drew his sword from its sheath with a shaking hand. "Kellach, can you do that levitate spell again?"

"Yes, but—"

"So do it!" Driskoll commanded, his voice taking on a sudden ring of authority.

"The spell will only levitate two people!" Kellach began weaving his hands in the air, beginning the spell preparations.

From the other end of the alley, Torin lowered his sword in challenge, his eyes drifting over the trio without recognition.

"Do you want to save our fathers or not?" Driskoll yelled.

"Of course we do!" Moyra cried, her fingers gripping Driskoll's jacket.

Driskoll turned toward her. "Then, go," he said softly. "You've got the antidote recipe. Kellach has the know-how to make it. You can come back for me later and get me out of jail. By then, you'll have the antidote, and our dads' minds will be their own."

"But, Driskoll, if we leave you, the watchers won't take you to jail. They're under the medusa's control." Moyra met Driskoll's eyes. "They'll take you straight to . . . *her!*"

"There's no time. You've got to get out of here and save the city. We don't have a choice." Driskoll's dark eyes were serious, and his voice was steady.

"Driskoll! No!" Moyra cried.

"He's right," Kellach said, wrapping his arm around Moyra's waist as he finished his spell. Kellach and Driskoll locked eyes. "Good luck."

"I don't need luck. I keep *telling* you that." With a grin, Driskoll saluted his brother with his sword and turned to face Torin alone.

Kellach muttered a few words, and he and Moyra flew upward, away from Driskoll. Kellach looked down beneath their feet and saw watchers surrounding Driskoll on every side, led by Torin and Arren.

Kellach gripped the roof of a nearby building and drew them swiftly onto it, letting the spell drop as they fell upon the tiles. They looked down.

Driskoll's weapon clanged, steel on steel, as his sword met with his father's larger blade. Torin easily disarmed his son, stealing away the very sword he had only recently given him. He pressed Driskoll against the wall, bearing forward as if to kill him. But at the last moment, he paused.

"No, wait," Torin drew his sword back, a slow smile creeping across his features. "I've got a better idea."

The watchers surrounding them in the alley stared with empty faces as Torin reached into his pouch and pulled out a vial. "We'll use the wizard's medicine."

The watchers guffawed, their laughter echoing from the warehouses around them. Torin grabbed his son. Driskoll wiggled, but he couldn't free himself from his father's steely grip. Taking hold of his hair, he tipped Driskoll's head backward and poured the liquid down his throat. A few seconds later, the boy slumped to the ground.

"Take him away." Torin grinned, and the laughter of the watch echoed in the night.

CHAPTER

17

"This is all your dragon's fault," Moyra moaned. "I told you. He told the medusa everything! He told her where we were! She sent the watch to get us."

"That's not possible." Kellach shook his head angrily. "Locky would never do that."

The two sat in Moyra's front room, hiding in Broken Town. Outside, the final day of the Promise Festival dawned with faint clouds across a purple red sky.

They had gotten little sleep that night. Kellach couldn't return back home after what had happened at the warehouse. So he had huddled on the cushions in Moyra's front room and listened to Breddo's howl from the back bedroom all night long.

Kellach rubbed the back of his neck wearily and stood, leaving the book on venoms on the table. He ambled over to the window and peered outside. People walked the city streets, filling the air with happy laughter. Still, there was something chilling about it all.

Kellach sighed. "Driskoll's going to be fine. He's gotten

himself out of rougher scrapes than this. I'm sure of it."

"Where did that dragon go after we looked at the statue in Main Square, Kellach? Why did he show up at the warehouse right before the watch?"

"I don't know," Kellach muttered.

"We can't trust him. He's a horrible little spy, working for that medusa. It's time you realized the truth, Kellach. It's his fault we were caught, and it's his fault that Driskoll's in trouble. We can't trust that dragon!"

Kellach lowered his head against the window. "You're right," he said quietly, anger burning in his voice. "If I see Lochinvar again, I'll . . . I'll send the dragon away."

"Or take him apart. He's little more than a collection of treacherous nuts and bolts," Moyra said fiercely. "I still say that Driskoll will be very lucky if he can get away. He's in a lot of trouble, Kellach."

The image of Torin pinning Driskoll against the wall flashed before Kellach's eyes. He shook his head to clear it of such thoughts.

"He'll be fine. He's always fine. Any minute, he'll be walking through that door, telling us all about his big adventure. Probably in rhyme." Kellach stuck out his chin and refused to consider any other possibility.

Kellach walked back to Moyra and the book. Leaning over it, he smoothed the page with the antidote. He read the directions once more. "This is really complex. I wish we could ask Zendric to help."

"Well, we can't. We know he's working with a medusa, Kellach, and that means he can't be trusted."

"You don't understand. I can't complete the formula alone."

"Why not?" Moyra looked up, the worry clear on her face.

"Entwistle, mother's root, echacia, yam, and black agate—we can buy those in the marketplace. Yew breath will be more difficult, but I know there are several merchants in the city who may have it in stock." Kellach rubbed the back of his neck again. "But medusa tears. For all I know, the potion needs the real thing."

"From what the legends say, medusas are terrible, cruel, and entirely evil. I don't think we should take that line of the antidote literally. I'm sure they can't cry. So that entry must refer to another herb, or something else entirely." Moyra stared down at the book on the table, trying to read it upside down. "Where can we research that?"

Kellach said mournfully, "Zendric would know. I bet he's got a hundred books that would tell us."

"Kellach, not this again," Moyra kicked at the paper, grumbling. "We can't go to Zendric."

Kellach threw up his hands. "Well, then, it's hopeless."

The young wizard paced across the room, then sat down on the floor beside the fireplace, closing his eyes. He found his thoughts returning to the carvings on the first statue, and to the symbols that Moyra had copied from the second one. The first was obviously part of a riddle, but were the carvings on the second statue the answer?

If only Locky were here, he could read the symbols Moyra had copied from the second statue and have the answer. If they could just solve the riddle, maybe they could find out what the medusa was holding over Zendric and free his friend from her power. Then Zendric would be free to help them make the antidote and release the town from the medusa's terrible control.

Maybe he could figure out how to read the second set of carvings on his own. Kellach copied the symbols from Moyra's notes on the ash of the fireplace hearth, trying to see any logical pattern to the symbols.

A scratching on the window drew Kellach's attention, and his head snapped up. "What was that?" He turned his head, listening.

"What was wh—"

Moyra heard the scratching, and she shifted to her feet in a flash. "They must have found us."

She reached for the little dagger on the table, gripping it in an instant. "Quick, check the door. If it's the watch, then we'll run out the back."

Kellach shook his head. "I don't think they're looking for us anymore. They're too drugged to remember where you live. At this point, I seriously doubt they even remember what they were looking for."

Kellach crawled to the window and risked a look outside. His eyes widened.

"Moyra, open the door."

"What?"

"Do it, do it quickly!" Kellach scrambled away from the window.

Moyra darted over to the door, unlocked and opened it.

In flew a streak of silver, whirring and chittering excitedly. The dragon whirled toward the ceiling, swooping through the room before swinging in a circle above Kellach's head. A slash of blue fabric hung between the dragon's claws, fluttering as he leaped and bounded back and forth around the room.

"It's that creature!" Moyra looked displeased, her nose

wrinkling. "Kellach, we have to get rid of him." Lochinvar landed on Kellach's arm, throwing his head back and howling in animated despair.

Moyra clapped her hands over her ears. "Stop him! Stop him! He's going to make everyone outside curious, and then the watch will come for sure!"

She kicked the door closed with one foot, running to the window to jerk the curtains back over the panes.

"Locky! Locky!" Kellach tried to soothe the mechanical animal. He grabbed the dragonet's head and set him down on the table, forcing his violet eyes to lock with his own. "Look what he's got in his claws."

"What is it?"

Kellach pulled the scrap of fabric free. "This is from Driskoll's jacket."

Moyra tugged the curtains together, cursing softly as the silver dragon's cries diminished. She peered out through the windowpanes, searching the road for any sign of the watch. "I don't think anyone noticed. The sound of the festival is enough to keep any of the tourists from paying attention. But Kellach," Moyra turned and glared, "he can't stay!"

"Driskoll," Kellach said softly, staring into the dragon's eyes. "Where is my brother?" Lochinvar's thoughts flickered into Kellach's head like a flowing stream, images rushing one after the other in a confusing deluge. "I think . . . I think he's been with Driskoll!"

Moyra took a half step forward, unwillingly. "Driskoll? But where? Where did they take him?"

"I can't understand. There's too much. Calm down, Locky."

Kellach tried to soothe the little beast, stroking the silver scales of its neck and whispering in gentle tones. Still, the images from the mechanical beast's mind were fractured, twisted by excitement and confused, gushing forth all at once in a mess of imagery.

"Kellach, I told you, we can't trust Lochinvar."

"We have no other choice, Moyra. And if he can help us find Driskoll, then I'm willing to try." Kellach persuaded Lochinvar to stop flapping his wings and crooning, slowly convincing the mechanical creature to listen. Even Moyra was silent, dropping down onto a nearby chair with a mutinous stare.

Slowly, Kellach began to sort through Locky's memories, drawing out the ones he needed. As he began to understand the little dragon's tale, Kellach stumbled, then sat heavily onto the chair beside the table. He dropped his head in his hands.

"What? What is it?"

Kellach looked up. "Driskoll's been turned to stone."

Moyra gasped, covering her hands with her mouth. "Stone? Oh no!" Despite herself, she blurted out, "I told him this would happen! The medusa got him!"

Kellach clamped his lips together tightly. In his mind, he saw again the image of his brother standing, steadfast, in the alley as the watchers rushed him.

"He was so brave." Kellach whispered, wishing that Driskoll could hear him now.

Moyra turned on the dragon, fire in her eyes. "Lochinvar! You've got to lead us to the medusa. You've seen her. You know where she is, and if she's got Driskoll . . . "

"Locky says that the medusa doesn't have him anymore."

Lochinvar chirruped again, and Kellach looked confused.

"He's asking me what the letters are?" Kellach followed the dragonet's gaze and saw the symbols he had been drawing on the floor. "Oh!"

Moyra said it before Kellach could. "The symbols from the second statue. Lochinvar will read them!"

Kellach nodded, and Moyra scrambled to pull the piece of paper toward them, upon which she'd drawn the patterns that she'd seen on the second statue.

"What does it say, Locky?" Kellach leaned forward eagerly, holding the dragon over the page and encouraging the dragonet to take an interest in the letters. Lochinvar concentrated, his chirps and burbles strangely silent. His wedge-shaped head went still as he stared down at the paper, wings folded along his silver-scaled back.

Kellach closed his eyes. One by one, new images began to trickle into his mind. "Paper, give me a piece of paper, Moyra."

She darted up out of the chair and grabbed the medusa's journal. She opened the journal to a blank page. "Use this. I've got charcoal, too, from the fire." Moyra placed a blackened stick in front of Kellach's wandering hand. She guided his hand to the charcoal so that he could transcribe Locky's thoughts.

Kellach opened his eyes and scanned the paper. "Yes! There's the last line of the first riddle. It's 'the west.' " Kellach recited,

I send a plea that you might seek
a serpent's secret nest.
Where north is north
The needle spins
And east becomes THE WEST.

Kellach grimaced. "Well, that doesn't help much."

"What's the rest of the second riddle? Is there something there that will help us?" Moyra asked.

Kellach twisted the journal toward her so that she could read it too.

The west.
To make a path that you can see,
At this you must not fail
A dish of water, red quartzite,
and

Moyra scratched her head. "That makes no sense either."

"It's a riddle. We need to puzzle it out . . . 'To make a path that you can see.'" Kellach leaned back in his chair and closed his eyes. "What's a path that you can see?"

"A road? A trail? I don't know."

"No, I think it's supposed to mean something that tells you where to go. Like directions. A map . . ."

"A . . . a compass?" Moyra said.

Kellach sat up so quickly he nearly fell out of his chair. "That's it! The riddle is telling us how to make a compass—a magical compass. Red quartzite is a common ingredient for magical compasses. I'm sure of it. 'North is north . . . the needle spins.' It all adds up." Kellach smiled triumphantly.

"Can we find what we need to make the compass?" Moyra sounded hopeful.

"I think so." Kellach tapped the paper importantly, running

his finger under each item as he ticked it off in his mind. "Red quartzite is a magical stone. It has unusual properties. Zendric never lets me experiment with it because it's so unreliable."

"Oh! I've seen that in the market. My mom's friend sells it."

"Great! Then we need water and a bowl. Those are all easy to find. But . . . " Kellach's triumphant smile faded.

"It's still not finished!" Moyra clutched the side of the table, upset. The dragon stared at her with anguished eyes. "There's obviously something missing at the end of this stanza. It ends with 'and.' "

"That's all there was. You wrote it down yourself, Moyra. We got everything," Kellach's tone was despondent. He gently caressed Lochinvar's shoulders. "The only answer is that there must be more carvings somewhere."

"But where? Have you seen any other statues?"

Kellach shook his head.

"Without the rest of this riddle, we can't help Driskoll. We can't find out what the medusa's holding over Zendric, and, without Zendric, we can't make the antidote to the wyrmserum, and the people of Curston will be doomed."

"Hang on. We're missing something here." Kellach paused, his brow furrowing as he thought out loud. "Let's start with our basic assumptions. We're assuming that the medusa who is creating these statues is the same one who is blackmailing Zendric. She is making this riddle to lead someone to her hiding place," Kellach frowned. "I don't think that's it, though. It doesn't make sense. Zendric's visitor has been able to move around the city pretty much at will. She was staying at the Stein and Silence. She's not exactly hiding."

"But who is creating the statues—and the message?" Moyra asked.

Kellach didn't seem to hear her. He patted Locky's head absently as he continued to think aloud.

"Yes, the riddle is in the medusa's language, but that doesn't mean she wrote it herself. I bet it's not a message *from* her, but a message *to* her. It's like a treasure map. It leads to something she's been looking for."

"Lochinvar knows her language too," Moyra chimed in. "Maybe he's the one making these statues?"

Clockwork gears spun and whirred as Lochinvar raised his head. His eyes narrowed. He seemed to be considering whether to nip Moyra on the wrist. Moyra pulled her hand away.

"Don't be ridiculous! Locky would never do something like that. He's just as worried about Driskoll as we are. This doesn't make any sense to him either." Kellach sighed.

"I'm worried about Driskoll too, but . . . " Suddenly, comprehension dawned in Moyra's eyes. "Driskoll!" She stood up quickly, grabbing Kellach's sleeve so hard that she nearly dislodged Lochinvar. "Kellach, Locky told you that Driskoll had been turned to stone. He'd been turned to stone!"

It only took Kellach a few seconds to follow her thought. "The third statue. It's Driskoll!" Eagerly, he asked the mechanical dragon, "Locky, Driskoll? Did you see any carvings on Driskoll?" The dragon shook his head, but that didn't dampen Kellach's excitement. "He says no, but I think Lochinvar never really got a good look at Driskoll after he was turned to stone."

"Ask him to tell us where Driskoll is! If we can find Driskoll, then we might find the third clue."

"Locky, where is Driskoll? *Ow!*" Kellach winced and brought his hands up to his ears.

"What now?"

"He's really upset. I can't tell what he's saying." Kellach frowned, trying to sort out the little dragon's chirps and howls. "He didn't see where they took Driskoll. He was in . . . I think he was in Driskoll's pocket. He's telling me about a dark place, something like being wrapped in a blanket. Locky, calm down. Talk slower."

With difficulty, Kellach soothed the little dragon, petting his wings gently. "That's better. He's telling me everything he saw . . . peeking out a pocket, and harsh voices: a male and a young female. Then, he says that he crawled out just as Driskoll was turned to stone." Kellach's face fell with guilt and worry.

Moyra cried, "But where is he?"

"There's a wagon, and a crate. I think Driskoll was boxed up after he was turned to stone." Trying to steer the dragon's mind through the confusing events, Kellach gathered, "The crate was on a wagon, but Locky knocked it off the back. Now it's in a ditch somewhere . . . He's describing a tree, blackened by lightning, with a broken branch."

Kellach's face brightened. "Hey! I think I know that tree. It's growing right outside the city, just past the Westgate. If Locky hadn't knocked the crate off the wagon, Driskoll would be half-way to the northern cities by now." The young wizard caressed the dragonet's head gently. "Good job, Locky."

"I'll get the red quartzite and meet you at the Westgate," Moyra said.

"But what about your ankle?

Moyra grabbed her jacket from the hook beside the door. "It's still a bit sore, but I'll be fine." She wiggled her foot at him to prove it.

Kellach picked up Lochinvar, steadying the weary dragon on his shoulder. "All right. I'll get the bowl and the water. Once we know what else the compass needs, we can make it and follow it. I think it's going to lead us to whatever the medusa is looking for. We can use that to undo the hold she has over Zendric. And force her to free him! It's the only way to save my dad, and your father. And all of Curston."

But Moyra didn't hear him. She was already running out the door.

CHAPTER

18

The Westgate stood wide open. Kellach and Moyra wove through the crowd of tourists and traders entering the city. They stared as two watchers sang childhood songs, lying against an overturned wagon and using their swords as puppets. The two men laughed, a horrible, sluggish sound.

There was only one watcher guarding the gate, asleep against the posts of the high wall. He was snoring so loudly that it drowned out the beat of horses' hooves along the road beside him. A half-eaten cinnamon bun lay in the watcher's hand, his mouth smeared with rich icing. Kellach and Moyra exchanged worried glances as they tiptoed past the sleeping watcher.

"This is awful," Moyra said. "Curston's in worse shape than we thought. I don't think we have much time."

Kellach nodded, and they hurried past the gate and onto the road beyond.

The road to the west was overgrown on both sides, with wagon tracks cut deeply into the earth from the long trains of visitors to Curston for the festival. Brilliant yellow dandelions shimmered in the sunlight, spreading their yellow glow within the shadows of the taller weeds. They dotted the hillside like specks of the sun fallen to earth, glimmering all around Curston. Kellach kicked at the brushes as they tromped along the road, his eyes eagerly scanning for any sign of the blackened tree and the hidden crate.

High in the air above them, a tiny silver spark caught the sunlight. Lochinvar darted here and there, and at last let out a crow of triumph. Kellach looked up and saw the dragonet performing loop-de-loops across the clouds.

"He must be able to see the crate from up there," Moyra pointed to the shining creature. With a sharp dive, Lochinvar began to herd the two companions toward their goal.

At last, Kellach caught sight of dark wood in the middle of a stand of healthy oak trees. The bottom branch of the tree hung down at an angle like a broken arm.

"There's the tree!" Kellach called. He raced over a thicket to get to it, nearly stumbling into the ditch at the base of the tree.

Inside the ditch, he caught sight of pale wood underneath a mass of green shrubbery. He ran his hands over the edge of the crate as Moyra joined him.

"I think the lid's broken open a bit here." Between the two of them, they pushed away the brush and tugged the lid away.

It was hard to recognize Driskoll at first, his features strangely colorless and seemingly chiseled from solid marble. Driskoll's statue stood like a conquering champion, arms before him and a cloak unfurled around his outstretched legs. He held the hilt of his Promise Day sword in both hands, the point of the weapon rising above his head as he stared past the blade.

His clothing was blown by an unseen wind, hair swept back from his forehead. He had a serious, earnest look upon his face.

Moyra laughed. "He looks just like a hero. He would have liked that."

"It's not funny, Moyra," Kellach said softly.

Moyra's smile disappeared and she placed her hand on Kellach's shoulder. "We'll get Driskoll back. I promise you that."

Kellach tried to cover the faint tremor in his voice. "Of course we will."

He touched the statue gingerly, his finger sliding down the edge of Driskoll's cloak. "Look at that."

Along the curve of stone, the patterns of a strange language ornamented Driskoll's cloak like spiders crawling down over the wrinkles of the carved fabric.

"They look so strange," Moyra gulped, staring at the symbols. "I mean, I understood that the others . . . but Driskoll . . . poor Driskoll." She leaned in and touched Driskoll's face. "Do you think he can hear us?"

"No. I think it's like sleeping. He's just dreaming, there."

"It certainly looks like it. How strangely regal he seems." Moyra cocked her head. "It doesn't suit him."

Together, she and Kellach brushed the packing straw away from Driskoll's marble body. They dug around the base of the statue and the edges of his cloak until all the runes were clearly visible. Kellach looked at the symbols, grinning widely as he recognized them. "The next part of the riddle. I hope this is the end."

Lochinvar hummed on the edge of the crate, peering down curiously.

Moyra nodded. "Quick, then. Get Locky to read it, and let's see." Moyra handed him the medusa's journal and a piece of charcoal.

"Right." Kellach patted the dragon's head. He sat down and closed his eyes.

The dragonet skimmed the symbols happily, humming a tuneless, mechanical air that held little substance and less melody. Kellach didn't seem to notice. He was too busy concentrating on reading the nuances of the strange medusa script through Locky's eyes.

> one brass nail.
> Place a sun upon the stone,
> and you will swiftly see
> The secret of the stone is this:
> the light will follow me.

"That's it," Kellach's eyes flew open.

Moyra quickly scanned what he had written and whooped. "It's the end of the riddle! There are no more stanzas. The rhyme is complete."

Kellach smiled. "This should be all we need to know in order to solve the riddle, if we can just figure out what it means."

"A brass nail I can find for you." Moyra knelt in the dirt and pried a small tack from the sole of her shoe. "Here! That was easy enough."

The brass glinted in the bright light of day as she placed it into Kellach's hand. "But, how are we going to get a sun? I'm not tall enough to reach the sky!" Moyra shook her head.

"We'll never get this compass to work."

Kellach jumped to his feet. "You're just saying that because you aren't a wizard, Moyra!"

Reaching into his pack, he pulled out the bowl and a small waterskin. He poured water from the waterskin into the bowl then dropped the nail into the water.

"There's a special herb whose name means 'tiny sun' in the wizard's lexicon. And don't worry." He reached out to pluck one of the dandelions that dotted the hillside and shook it triumphantly. "It's as common as an everyday weed, and far closer than the sky."

"Wow! A dandelion!" Moyra said.

Kellach took the red quartzite stone from Moyra's hand, rubbing it with the dandelion before placing it in the water. To be certain, he floated several more of the fuzzy blossoms in the water, letting them fill the small wooden bowl with their golden glow.

There was an instant gleam within the bowl as the ingredients were all placed together, and then a bright light erupted from the red quartzite.

"It's working!" he shouted.

Kellach and Moyra peered into the bowl. The brass nail clung to the small crystal, spinning wildly and glowing red.

"Red quartzite is highly magical," Kellach whispered, watching the spell take hold. "I'm not sure what's going to happen."

At that moment, the light became brighter, making the dandelions in the bowl glow like little golden boats upon the water.

The nail spun again, and a shaft of light slipped along its

length, pointing directly toward one side of the bowl. Kellach turned the bowl, but the glow remained, shining against one edge.

"Tell me again," Moyra looked down at the bowl with suspicion, "How exactly is that thing working?"

"Like any compass, it's drawn to point at something: the magnetic north or the closest ore deposit. Whatever the compass is keyed to, it continues to point toward the same direction. No matter what's in between."

"And what's making that thing point that way?" she asked skeptically.

"Red quartzite is a stone that is innately magical. When we put the other items in, the stone made a magical field, like a spell. That's what's making the light. The compass—" Kellach stumbled over his words, trying to find a way to explain in lay terms. It seemed incredibly simple to him, but to Moyra, the idea was a confusing tangle of metaphysical threads. "If I had a book, I could tell you what it is tracking, probably a unique metal deposit, or an unusual plant. Whatever it is, the person who made the riddle knew that they had the only source of that in the area or the largest source. They knew that the red quartzite would point the way.

"Like a normal compass, the light on the stone will continue to lean in a certain direction. Even when I turn the bowl, the light stays pointing that way." Kellach looked up, over the light, and saw that it headed farther away from the city, south, along a small stream. "We've got our compass."

"Now, all we have to do is follow it," Moyra said, covering the stone Driskoll with the crate lid. "Sorry that you can't come,

Driskoll, but you're far too heavy for us to lift, much less tote you back to town." She grinned at the stone statue within the crate, patting the lid back on and carefully making sure it was hidden within the weeds. "Sleep well, and we'll be back for you before the fireworks begin."

CHAPTER

19

Kellach and Moyra walked south, their steps beating in rhythm on the ground. There was no path, no road, only the light against the side of the bowl to show the way. Over small scrub-brush hills they marched, skittering up through the tangled, dry weeds.

Moyra paused to look ahead, shielding her eyes from the sun. "We're not far from the south wall," she began, even as Kellach let out a whistle. "What?

"The compass. It's gone haywire."

Moyra scrabbled down a slippery hillock, her feet digging into the dirt to slow her tumble. "What's gone wrong?"

Kellach walked forward, then backward, then once to each side. "The light's going in circles as we walk around. We must be so close to whatever this compass is pointing at, that the needle is spinning. Look! It goes round and round when I stand here, as if this is the spot we were looking for. But it can't be," he looked at the grass and weeds in dismay. "There's nothing here."

"Maybe there's something buried. Or underground?"

"Of course!" Kellach looked down at the bowl, then started pacing the area. "It's got to be here, somewhere." His sandy blond hair bobbing, Kellach nodded. "That's the logical answer."

His eyes took in a cluster of strange bushes. "Look! There are footprints in the dirt heading right into the bushes. You can see the indentations from here, if you look carefully. That bush isn't native. The bushes have been replanted there. They're deliberately hiding something."

"That means someone's interested in keeping it secret." She inched forward, trying to get a better look.

"And that means," Kellach smiled, "We're in the right place." Kellach handed the bowl to Moyra, who grasped it cautiously.

He bent down and tugged at the brush, pulling the limbs and vines away from the hillside. "Look!"

Behind the concealing plants, there was a small opening into the hillside, just large enough for a person to walk through if crouched over. It was old, and the thick wooden planks that supported the opening were covered in spider webs and vines. But the ground that led into the earth was clean, swept almost bare by the passage of many feet.

"It's a mine shaft," Moyra breathed softly, her face illuminated by the golden glow of the compass. The steady shine from the red quartzite lit the side of the bowl, reflecting against the golden dandelions that floated on the water.

"I heard there were a few around Curston. The hills around here were mined—not for long, of course. Not after they found the Dungeons of Doom."

Moyra held the bowl like fine china as she carefully approached the entrance. "Have you ever thought that this entire thing could be a trap?"

"It might be. But we have to try. We took an oath to protect Curston. We've got to do whatever we can."

"You're right, Kellach." She stuck out her chin stubbornly. "We're Knights of the Silver Dragon. It's our duty."

Moyra carefully slipped into the tunnel, noting the delicate work of vines and spider webs that covered the entrance. "This is well done. Obviously, whoever constructed the blind didn't expect it to ever be uncovered. They really didn't want this shaft to be found."

Kellach felt a strange tugging on his shoulder and looked up. Lochinvar fluttered his wings, eyes whirling in panic. He stared into the mine, hissing, and then tugged on Kellach's robes once again.

"What's wrong, Locky?" Kellach asked. As the dragon continued his frantic struggles, Kellach pulled him down.

"Are you worried about going underground? It's just a hole, Locky. What are you so frightened about?" But the little creature continued to hiss and fight, flapping his wings widely and extending his clockwork neck. Gears shifted within his body as he strained to pull Kellach away from the mine, whimpering and speaking in broken tongues.

"What's he doing?" Moyra said crossly from just within the ancient shaft. "Shut him up, Kellach! It's echoing down here like crazy."

"I'm trying," Petting the dragonet had no effect, nor did Kellach's whispered words of encouragement. "All right, Lochinvar, all right!"

Kellach finally let go, and his dragonet sprang into the air. Lochinvar clung to the vines at the entrance of the hole, his amethyst eyes catching the sunlight like faceted jewels. "Stay outside, then," Kellach ordered. "But if we don't come back by nightfall, go and get help."

"Who is he going to get? Torin? Pralthamus?" Moyra snorted, turning her back and continuing into the mine. "If he's afraid, then let him stay. There won't be much room for flying where we're going, anyway."

Kellach patted the silver-scaled dragonet a final time, finding it hard to ignore the creature's worried croon. "Take care, fellow." Kellach sighed. Turning away, he followed Moyra into the hillside.

Ancient wooden supports held the crumbling roof above their heads, the thick boards eaten by termites and eroded by years and floods. It unnerved Kellach to see dust and fragments of stone falling softly in front of them.

As the vine-laden opening receded into the darkness behind them, Kellach wished for a moment that none of this had happened. Poor Driskoll. It seemed so long ago that they had awakened, eager to make their way into Main Square and see all the traders visiting from faraway lands. "Maybe my brother wasn't such a chicken after all," he whispered regretfully, kicking a stone against the side of the mine shaft.

The earth beneath his feet was hard and unyielding. The passages were taller than Breddo's secret passage to the prison, but thinner. The only light in the tunnel was the quiet flicker of the compass-stone within the watery bowl, casting strange, liquid reflections of red and purple against the walls.

After a few moments of walking, Moyra gestured to Kellach to stop. She handed the bowl to him and pressed her fingers lightly against the stone floor. "Aha," she whispered. "There's a trap here. It looks like some sort of putty has been molded over the floor to hide something beneath. Maybe a fire bomb."

"Fire bomb?" Kellach scooted closer, jerking his foot away from a stone that had snagged his pants. As he did, he heard a faint, but distinct click.

"Yes, the kind of trap that sets off an explosion—" Moyra stopped, her fingers freezing over the puttied floor. "Oh no. It's just been triggered."

Kellach groaned, remembering the slight tug of the stone against his leg. "Oops."

"Kellach!" Moyra's hands flew over the floor, watching in horror as the ground began to crack. She jumped to her feet. "Forward or backward?" she said frantically.

"*Uh . . .*" For once in his life, Kellach couldn't think of anything. His face reddened.

"Forward or backward? Which way do we jump?" Moyra sounded panicked, as the putty on the floor crumbled away. "We can't stay here. The floor is going to explode! Which way?"

"Forward!" Kellach yelled, leaping across the three-foot block of floor that was crumbling and smoking. Moyra jumped beside him, covering her face from the fumes that were already beginning to pour through the cracks in the floor.

They raced down the tunnel, trying desperately not to breathe in the yellowish fumes. The light of the magic compass warbled crazily, its glow skittering across the walls and flashing into Kellach's eyes.

Blinded by the fog, Moyra crashed into Kellach. He reached out to stop himself from falling. But instead of stone, his hand met a sheet of cloth hiding another passageway. He fell forward through the cloth, his palms slamming onto a sloped floor.

The bowl crashed against the stone. It shattered, and the red quartzite was flung forward, vanishing out of sight into the smoke.

The light instantly went out.

Kellach rolled down the passageway. Sparks flew across his vision as he tumbled downhill along a narrow corridor. He braked against the wall with his hands, feeling the stone scuff the skin, rubbing it raw before he eventually skidded to a stop. Moyra landed upside down just behind him, her shoulders wedged against the wall.

Through slightly blurred vision, Kellach saw that he was in a stone chamber, a natural widening of the mine shaft that was large enough to hold several small cots and a number of chairs surrounding a table. The chamber was still softly lit.

He glanced back at Moyra and saw that the crevice at the top of the slope was covered by a black rectangle of fabric, blocking all light from the main passageway above.

"What . . . the world . . . we gots here?" A voice, slow and halting, was hideously familiar. Kellach tried to clear his head, pushing against the wall to right himself. Kellach's vision blurred, stunned from the fall. He desperately shook his head to try to see more.

Looking up again, he saw a tremendous bulk rising from a chair across the room. The torch that hung in a small sconce on the far side of the room was darkened as someone massive moved between the light and Kellach's eyes. Whatever was coming toward him lurched dangerously closer, muttering in a rough voice, "Two little rats. Have to stamp them out, boys! Like with all the rats, yeah." Suddenly, Kellach realized that he knew the voice.

Gult.

CHAPTER

20

Kellach shook his head again, certain he was imagining things. What would Gult be doing down here?

But as Kellach's vision cleared, he saw the giant watcher approaching, and he knew he was real.

Worse, he saw five other men rising around the room. Two of them he recognized—it was Tonna and Sedrick, the watchers who guarded the door to Watchers' Hall. Their eyes were dull, and they hardly noticed the swords that they drew from their sides. The other three were laughing. One was short and stocky, with red hair. The other was tall and lanky. The third man wore a tight cap on his head. They were the bandits that had attacked Kellach and Driskoll at Arren's warehouse!

With a start, Kellach realized why their faces had looked familiar during the warehouse fight. The bandits were watchers, too, who worked at the prison with Guffy. But, why then, had they been chasing the medusa? Maybe the medusa wasn't the one who was trying to control Curston's watch after all? But if not her, then who? Gult?

It didn't make any sense!

The watchers circled behind Gult, staggering forward with the sluggish gait of drugged men.

Moyra kicked at Kellach as she tried to flip upright. Her head was stuck beneath Kellach's arm. She was all but upside down in the hallway, and Kellach had no choice but to move forward in order to give her the room she needed to get up.

Two against six, Kellach thought, and one of the six seemed as tall and as broad as the mountain that surrounded them.

Gult sluggishly drew his mace from his belt hook, running the wooden handle through his fingers.

"Get them, boys!" The men swarmed forward, and Kellach hopped to his feet to avoid their rush. But he wasn't fast enough.

Tonna and Sedrick grabbed Kellach's legs. One of the bandits hurled his ale mug at the boy's head.

Kellach shouted, trying to duck and jump at the same time, and landed in a tumble with the two men on the floor.

Above him, the ale mug shattered against the stone wall.

Moyra lunged, plunging her dagger into Tonna's leg. The man howled. He tried to kick at her. But she was faster. Moyra quickly rolled away.

"This is like fighting bowls of jelly!" Moyra shouted. "Dangerous, well-armed bowls of jelly!"

Kellach slid out from under Sedrick. He scrambled away, reaching for the spell components at his waist.

Behind Kellach, Moyra kicked over the table where the men had been sitting. Cards, ale, and chips flew everywhere. A glass full of ale sprayed Gult in the face.

"Get them!" he yelled sluggishly.

The bandits looked at Gult and snarled. But they charged anyway.

Kellach called, "Why are you taking orders from him? He never does anything but sit behind a desk and eat twice the rations any of you receive! I thought you were watchers, not dogs."

"Oh, great, Kellach. Get them mad." Moyra leaped backward. She tried to hurl one of the benches at the three men rushing forward.

They dodged.

Moyra leaped toward the closest one, grabbing his wrist as she ducked beneath his arm.

The man was running too fast to stop. He flew over her back and fell to the floor, unconscious.

"That one's for my dad!" she shouted.

The bandit with the tight cap ran toward her. She crouched beneath his wild swing and kicked viciously at his knee. It connected with a crunch, and he fell, gripping his leg. It would only hold him for a moment, but that should be enough.

"They're so slow. It's almost like they want us to hit them!" Moyra crowed.

"Don't get cocky!" Kellach shouted in return. "They're still dangerous!"

Kellach began an incantation as Gult lumbered toward him. The huge watcher did not bother to include himself in the fight against Moyra.

"Leave the girl," he shouted at the watchers. "Get the wizard!" He pounded straight toward Kellach.

"Moyra, help!" Kellach cried.

"Hang on, I'm working on it!"

Tonna and Sedrick surrounded Moyra. They tried to grab her, but she dodged them. They had knives similar to her own dagger, but theirs were larger and less agile.

Tonna tried to slide his knife into her rib cage. Moyra grabbed his wrist and pulled forward.

The dagger stabbed Sedrick in the hip. Sedrick screamed in pain.

Moyra winced, wishing there had been some other way.

"I . . . ," Tonna began, hair falling into his eyes. Sedrick roared in anguish and he plunged his own dagger into Tonna's shoulder. Blood sprayed from the wound. Tonna gasped.

"You're the enemy!" Sedrick staggered to his feet. He grabbed Tonna's belt and slammed a sucker punch into his midsection.

"Gult said to get you! And I'm gonna!"

Completely forgetting Moyra, the two began to fight in earnest, their blades flashing in the torchlight.

"The drug's completely taken them over," Moyra yelled to Kellach. "They don't even know who's who anymore!"

But there was no time for Kellach to reply. Gult lifted his mace to crush Kellach's skull. Kellach's raised his hands, and fire sprayed from his fingertips directly toward Gult's face.

Gult reacted swiftly. He grabbed hold of the stocky, red-haired watcher standing next to him and shoved the man into the blaze. The fire lit his red hair on fire. The man screeched. He dropped his weapon to the ground and smacked his head violently to put out the flames.

Gult burst into horrible laughter. "Lookit you! Now your hair's really fire red!"

With a quick motion, Kellach grabbed a mug of ale and

dumped the contents over the burning man's head.

"Thanks," the watcher whimpered. Smoke poured from his burned hair, and ale trickled down over his face and ears.

"No problem," replied Kellach. He swung the now empty mug as hard as he could. It thumped against the watcher's temple, and the man went down in a soggy heap.

Gult roared, his mace crashing into the wall beside Kellach. Kellach dropped the mug and ran, dodging past Moyra and over the upturned table. He was no match for the much larger watcher, and he didn't look forward to even a single bone-crushing stroke from that bronze mace.

"Moyra!"

"Still working on it!" she yelled.

Kellach looked as the bandit with the cap got up from the floor and started toward her again. Moyra climbed onto one of the benches that stood against the wall behind the upturned table. As his sword flashed beneath her, she kicked out wildly. One kick connected with the watcher's chin. The man crumpled to the floor.

Gult backed Kellach into a corner. Kellach stumbled and fell. Gult laughed, a hoarse, guttural sound. He raised his mace to strike before Kellach could draw another spell against him.

"What is this?" A sharp voice cracked through the noise of battle.

Gult paused in his attack as if time had stopped for a moment.

A man in light blue robes stepped into the chamber. He looked like a king walking onto the battlefield. He held a small girl by the hand, her face hidden beneath a dark hood.

"Arren!" Moyra gasped.

CHAPTER

21

W retched children," Arren snarled. The little girl by his side pulled down on his hand trying to break his grip. But his hand was stronger, and she was forced to toddle beside him.

"You have broken the sanctity of my office, sticking your noses where they are most unwanted, and now you violate my private laboratory. I can't imagine how brats such as you ever survived this long without being thrown into the depths of Curston's prisons." Arren gloated. "Well, don't worry. We'll soon rectify that.

"Or perhaps I'd enjoy having two reminders of my victory decorating the walls of my new office when I take control from that idiot Pralthamus. Already, he is signing warrants that will enforce martial law upon the city. Poor Pralthamus," he said scornfully. "What a trusting fool he's been."

"With enough wyrmserum, anything is possible, eh, Arren?" Kellach rubbed his bruised jaw.

Arren stared down his hawklike nose at Kellach. "You've done well, boy. Zendric taught you well, didn't he?"

"Zendric is a powerful wizard. When he finds out what you're doing, he'll stop you." Kellach pushed up from the floor, but Gult haphazardly kicked the young wizard back down.

"Zendric is powerless to stop me. You, however—" Arren's eyes were chips of cold, gray stone. "Do you know how close you came to destroying all that I have worked for?" Arren stood over Kellach, sparing only a glance at Moyra. His cruel eyes were scathing, lip curled in a gesture of infinite disgust.

Kellach grimaced. "You poisoned the cinnamon buns and passed them out among the watch as gifts for Promise Day. Because it's the festival, they wouldn't think to ask where the pastries had come from, and the city's too busy for the watchers to realize what was happening to them. They're all spread out too thinly to be paying attention to one another. Once all the watchers were working for you, you were going to take over the city. But your men were chasing the medusa through the city, so it's obvious you're not working with her. There must be another medusa." Kellach's eyes flicked to the hooded girl at the alchemist's side. "Her."

Arren's lips twisted viciously. "Are you quite finished?"

"No." Kellach's tone was defiant, and he crawled to his knees as he continued. His eyes took in the small girl, her hood completely covering her face. Movement like small snakes twisted at the rear of her hood, and Kellach understood at last what she was. "That little girl is the medusa's daughter. You've kidnapped her, haven't you? You kept her in the prison for a while, working out the dosage of the wyrmserum on Breddo, until your men told you that the other medusa was in town. That was when you realized that it was unsafe to keep her in the city, and you moved her here. That journal we found in the prison was hers. She left it behind, hoping that someone would find it and discover what you were doing.

"That's why the other medusa is in the city. That's why Zendric is helping her. You've stolen her daughter in order to make the wyrmserum. I had no way to guess that you were so cruel."

Arren laughed out loud.

"That little girl . . . is a medusa?" Moyra whispered, aghast.

"Oh, very good, Kellach." Arren sneered, twisting the girl's wrist until she cried out in pain. "I've rescued this little beast from a lifetime among animals. Their culture is unformed and primitive, violent and cannibalistic. It isn't slavery to make a pet of such an animal, is it, Ssethedra?"

The hooded girl tried to pull away from Arren, saying nothing but obviously terrified. Arren shook her so hard that Kellach's teeth chattered.

Gult laughed sickly, his slow, drugged brain only now perceiving the little girl and her struggle.

"By this time tomorrow morning," Arren petted the little girl's hood, stroking her head through the material much as one might caress an animal, "Pralthamus will have signed the papers, enforcing martial law on the city. He will appoint me his captain at arms. With Pralthamus and all the watch under my control, they will enforce every law that I create for Curston. I think, for my first act of governance, I will raise taxes more than fifty times their current price. More money for me, you see. I'll leave this city a crumbling husk, and I will be a very rich man!" Arren's laugh was cold and cruel.

"Now, Ssethedra, behave," the alchemist said patronizingly as the girl struggled. Arren pressed down on her shoulders harshly, forcing the little girl to stand still. "You know full well why you're here."

Silently, she struggled to get away, forcing him to tug her across the stone floor until she stood in front of Kellach. "This one first, I think, and then you may also turn the girl to stone. Do try to make them pretty, my dear."

Arren stood directly behind the child. His claw-like hands gripped her shoulders like bird talons, sinking into the worn velvet of her cloak.

"I don't want to, I don't," the tiny girl whimpered. Her accent was thick and slurred with a natural hiss. Although she still wore the hood, Kellach could make out the outline of her features in its shadows.

Desperately, she tried to step away and twist her body out of Arren's sharp grasp, but the alchemist easily overpowered her. With a cruel grip on her shoulder, the alchemist drew back her hood.

Kellach turned his head away and squeezed his eyes shut. "Moyra! Close your eyes! Don't look at her!"

"Yes, do close your eyes," Arren approved. "Gult, hurt young Kellach's girlfriend until he chooses between opening his eyes or filling his ears with her screams."

"No!" Kellach shouted, but Gult laughed, and Kellach heard him marching toward his friend.

Moyra groaned as Gult knocked her to the gound. Kellach heard the swish of air as Gult's mace swirled over head.

"Kellach, don't do it!" Moyra shouted. "I can handle it."

"You know what you must do, Kellach," Arren murmured

reasonably. "It's really very easy. Just open your eyes. That's all, and Gult will leave your little friend alone."

"Okay! I'll do it." Kellach began to open his eyes.

"No!" Ssethedra stomped her little foot as hard as she could, catching Arren's toes angrily. The alchemist leaped back, staggering after the sudden pain, and Ssethedra darted forward.

"Get her!" Arren yelled.

Gult moved forward slowly, the wyrmserum dulling his reflexes. The watcher turned and raised his mace, preparing to strike the little girl.

From behind Ssethedra, Kellach saw Gult's pudgy, sadistic face shudder in horror as he looked down upon his target. The vipers of the young medusa's hair rose up about her head, hissing and writhing above her shoulders. Gult tried to scream, but it choked in his throat. His eyes widened and he froze in place, completely paralyzed by Ssethedra's eyes.

The watcher's skin grew pale, whitening to an unnatural pallor. He lowered his mace as the young medusa gestured. Cracks began to appear throughout his skin, veining the newly forming stone like marble.

Ssethedra reached for Gult's hand, gently moving the stone as it hardened and placing the watcher's arm in a heroic pose. Slowly, Gult's rippling fat seemed to harden. The stone gave him a definition that he never had before.

Kellach watched in fascination and horror as Ssethedra's fingers traced strange letters on the hardening stone, carving symbols into Gult's clothing. The forming stone rippled with her touch, easing itself into patterns dictated by the medusa's fledgling skill.

Before Kellach's eyes, the living Gult became a statue—its

eyes devoid of emotion, and its flesh cold and hard.

"Moyra! Keep your eyes closed!" Kellach scrambled to her side.

"What happened?

"Ssethedra's free. She got Gult."

Moyra wryly smiled, her hands over her eyes. "Maybe she'll get Arren next."

But they weren't safe yet.

Arren limped forward. "No hope of that, my dear," he called over to Moyra. "I do hate to disappoint you."

The alchemist grabbed Ssethedra by the arm, twisting the little girl's wrist sharply. "One thing your research must have failed to tell you. Those who are bitten by medusa—and live— are immune to that medusa's gaze for several days. Ssethedra has bitten me fairly recently, so I am immune to her stare. She can no longer harm me with her gaze."

Arren twisted his fingers into Ssethedra's viperous hair, ignoring the small snakes that struck helplessly at his hand. With a sharp jerk, he forced the little girl to turn around. Once more he pointed her toward Kellach. Ssethedra whimpered.

Kellach squeezed his eyes shut.

"I will forgive what you did to Gult, my dear," Arren snarled to the tiny medusa. "The man was a moron, and I will have little need of his service in my new rulership of Curston. But, if you disobey me again . . . "

A sharp crack echoed through the air, and although Kellach kept his eyes tightly closed, he could hear Ssethedra fall to the ground from the force of Arren's blow. He winced for her, feeling the pain of his own bruises.

Arren drew a long knife from a sheath within his robes, and both Moyra and Kellach heard the distinctive ring of steel. "This time, I will not ask others to do my work for me. If you do not do as I command, apprentice, I shall kill your friend myself.

"You have until the count of three, Kellach," the alchemist said scornfully. "And I assure you, I am not bluffing."

Kellach already knew that Arren would carry out his threat. With no choice, and little hope of escape, Kellach opened his eyes.

CHAPTER

22

Kellach drew in a sharp gasp of breath as Ssethedra's golden yellow gaze enveloped him. He caught a glimpse of a sweet, heart-shaped face with a snub nose and faintly greenish skin, surrounded by a wreath of quietly hissing snakes. He felt his muscles stiffening, and a terrible sense of cold gripped him to the core. Her eyes held him. Her yellow eyes.

Suddenly, a shrill whistle and a flash of silver erupted through the doorway.

Lochinvar flew through the room and threw himself at Ssethedra. The little girl screamed and turned away. Her arms reached up, trying to shield her face from the dragonet's needle-sharp talons.

As Ssethedra looked away, Kellach fell to the floor. "Locky!" he gasped.

Lochinvar attacked Ssethedra with a fury, beating her with his wings and slashing at her shoulders. With a scream, she hurled herself by the table, but the mechanical dragon chased after her, sweeping through fallen benches and over the table legs toward her.

He backed her into a corner, his claws slashing small, razor-sharp cuts in her robe as he breathed a cloud of smoke and sparks that nearly set the table on fire. Ssethedra shrieked—a shrill, horrified cry—hiding her face from the dragon's fiery assault. Furious that she would try to harm Kellach, Lochinvar continued his attack until the girl huddled in the corner, terrified of the creature.

Just then, Moyra screamed, and Kellach looked behind him, frightened of what he might find. Arren stood over Moyra, his knife moving to slash her throat.

Kellach's mind raced. He had to think of something . . . Scrambling to stand, he reached into his pouch and shouted, "Arren, over here!"

Arren's head whipped to the left.

Kellach drew a small lightning bug out of his pouch. *"Billeous luminum!"*

A ray of brilliant light burst into the room, flashing in Arren's face before the alchemist. For an instant, Arren was blinded.

The alchemist shook his head to clear it of the spell's terrible light. Moyra leaped to her feet. With a fierce rush, she grabbed one of the broken table legs and swung with all of her might. It struck Arren, doubling him over, and Moyra fell away from him toward the door. As she tried to run away, she tripped over one of the unconscious watchers on the floor. She landed heavily on the ground in front of the infuriated alchemist.

Sensing his opportunity, Arren surged forward, the knife glinting in his hand. Moyra screamed as she saw it descending toward her, unable to escape.

"No!"

Using all the strength in his body, Kellach threw himself toward the alchemist. His shoulder hit Arren in the stomach, folding the man in half around Kellach's body. Both of them fell to the ground in a heap, and Kellach slammed Arren's frail, birdlike hand into the ground once, twice, three times. The knife flew out of the alchemist's grip.

Arren struggled to his feet. Kellach whispered a few words and a burst of flame appeared in his hand. He slapped the fire against Arren's leg. It took Arren completely by surprise.

With a cry of pain, he jerked his leg away and stumbled backward. The sudden movement threw him off balance and he fell, hitting his head on the hard floor. He lay there, breathing, but limp against the stone.

For a moment, Kellach was as stunned as anyone, staring down at the alchemist's limp body.

"I did it!" he said to the suddenly quiet air. He grinned victoriously.

"Moyra, are you all right?" Kellach turned, a sickly feeling in his stomach.

She skittered across the floor, staring up at the corridor leading into the room. "*Um,* Kellach, we've got a problem."

A woman walked down the sloping corridor and stepped into the room. She wore a long velvet cloak in shimmering black-purple, the golden trim reflecting the torchlight along strange symbols at the robe's hem. Her footsteps were soft and silent, slippers making no sound across the stone as she advanced from the darkness toward them.

Although the hood of her robe was pulled sharply forward,

Kellach could hear the hissing beneath the thick velvet. Long jade green snakes slid out across the woman's shoulders, raising their viperous heads. Poison glistened along their fangs.

These were not Ssethedra's cute, asplike locks. This was the full deadly serpent mane of an adult medusa.

Lochinvar hissed on the other side of the room. His body whipped from side to side as he pinned Ssethedra to the ground. The girl shrieked. She clapped her hands over her eyes and huddled down in her tattered velvet robe.

The medusa turned. Her hands clenched in anger. She stalked forward toward the dragon, reaching up to remove the hood of her long velvet cloak.

"No! Lochinvar! Leave the little girl alone!" Kellach stretched out his hand toward the courageous little dragon. "Come here!" With a chirp, Lochinvar darted into the air above Ssethedra. He landed on Kellach's arm with a hiss. As Kellach petted the mechanical dragon, Lochinvar rubbed his head against his master's face, clearly grateful to see him alive and well.

"Kellach! Moyra!" the voice was familiar.

From behind the medusa, Driskoll darted into the room. "I wanted to come in right away, but Zendric wouldn't let me, not until Ssarine made sure it was safe!"

"Driskoll!" Moyra and Kellach both reached out to embrace him, throwing their arms around him and thumping his back vigorously.

"Are you all right?"

"How did you get turned to flesh again?"

The questions poured out simultaneously. All three kids laughed with joy.

"Zendric?" Kellach asked eagerly. "Did you say Zendric?"

"Well, someone had to get you out of this mess." From the doorway, the aged wizard smiled down at the three of them. "I can see we arrived a bit late."

Before Kellach could say anything, the little medusa rushed across the stone room and into the open arms of her mother. Although Ssarine's flowing cloak blocked their view of the little girl, Kellach could hear her happy cry.

"Mommy!"

23

Kellach clasped Driskoll's arm, and Moyra laughed aloud. Zendric watched the three reunite from the doorway, a quirky smile twisting his thin lips. On the far side of the room, the medusa mother embraced her child, the serpents of their hair twining happily.

Kellach realized that he was looking at them, and quickly turned away. "Don't look!" he said to his friends. "They might catch sight of us, and—" Driskoll held up his hand, and Kellach caught sight of a bandage wrapped around the fleshy palm. Taken aback, Kellach interrupted himself. "What happened to your hand?"

"Driskoll!" Moyra burst out, "Did you get chipped?"

"No, no. Ssarine—that's the medusa's name—turned me back all in one piece. But then she bit me."

Kellach nodded, understanding. "So you would be immune to her gaze. But you're still not immune to Ssethedra's, so don't look over there! But I'm guessing . . . "

Kellach glanced at Zendric, who stood smiling quietly by the doorway. "That . . . that must have been why Zendric's hand was injured, back when we went to see him at his tower. Ssarine had bitten him!"

"You're right, Kellach." Zendric drew up one of the fallen benches that littered the floor around the overturned table. "If she were a bit less busy, I'd introduce you to my old acquaintance, Ssarine. I see that you've already met her daughter. Good thing, too, because we've been looking for her rather desperately."

"Zendric, we've got to make an antidote to the wyrmserum. Arren's been feeding it to the watch—"

Moyra cut in, "And Daddy. He was the one Arren tested it on."

Kellach spoke hurriedly, "Arren used Gult to keep control up in the prison, and he fed the rest of the watchers wyrmserum in the cinnamon buns. We wanted to make an antidote, but it had a component that I couldn't re-create."

"You have the recipe for the antidote?" Zendric was frankly amazed. "But Arren would never have given that to you. I spent weeks researching to find it and couldn't discover the correct formula. How in the world did you discover it?"

"Moyra found it! She got it—ugh—" Kellach felt Moyra's foot come down on his, hard. She completed his sentence before he could.

"I was lucky enough to find a book." She smiled sweetly. "But we didn't have all the ingredients to put it together. It requires a rare ingredient: medusa tears."

"To counteract the medusa venom, of course! Well," Zendric raised his hands, chuckling at their rapid barrage. "I think we have plenty of that right here." And it was true. Ssarine held

Ssethedra close as the little girl wept in relief, her terrifying captivity at last over. "I'm certain that something can be arranged. With the formula you've, *ah,* discovered and Ssarine's help, we can create quite a bit of the antidote."

"She saved your life, didn't she?" Kellach asked quietly.

"In his youth, Zendric was quite the exploratory soul," the voice came from the corner, and Kellach shuddered before he could control himself. Ssarine pulled her hood back up over her head. She kept her child close, drawing the little girl's hood down to cover Ssethedra's features as well.

"Zendric and his fellows came to the island of my people. They thought they were clever enough to intrude and not be captured. Of course, they were only humans, and they were wrong." Ssarine stood a head taller than Zendric, her body lithe and willowy beneath the long velvet robe. She walked across the room with a firm, confident stride, keeping her daughter close by at her hip. "However, Zendric caught my eye. He was more intelligent than most of your species."

"Why, thank you, my dear," Zendric muttered with a hint of amusement.

"And I therefore determined that I would speak with him. I engineered to have him placed in my custody as a slave rather than have him given to the Royal Chef for preparation. In time, I released him."

"Royal Chef?" Moyra blanched. Driskoll, who had apparently heard the story once before, nodded in sympathy.

"Yes, well. Medusas are known for their cuisine, most of which specialize in human and elf dishes." Zendric cleared his throat uncomfortably. "Not meaning 'dishes of human and elven make,' but rather, 'dishes made of humans or elves.' "

Driskoll made a sour face, and Kellach shuddered.

Zendric continued, "When Arren's mercenary band kidnapped Ssethedra, Ssarine came to me for help. I was the only human she'd ever befriended, well, more or less befriended. The only one who would help her find her daughter."

"We can use the term 'befriended' for the sake of simplicity." Staring down at them from beneath her dark hood, Ssarine drew her daughter through the room to stand above Arren's prone form. "I do not, however, extend that same courtesy to all members of your species. Although, with Zendric's assistance, I have realized that there is inherent value in nonmedusan life, I still have no remorse and no pity for those who threaten my family." Her snakes hissed dangerously, and Ssethedra managed a timid kick at her fallen captor. Arren groaned on the floor, his eyes fluttering faintly, and then settled back into unconsciousness once more.

"Although she is nobly born, Ssarine's not like the rest of the medusas. Kellach," Zendric said gently. "After she allowed me to escape, she tried to teach her people that other races should be treated as equals." Zendric looked uncomfortable.

"My people did not agree, and I have been banned from the island," Ssarine finished. Her daughter pressed close against her hip, a faint whisper hissing from beneath her hood. Despite her thick robe, Ssarine stood with a regal bearing. The cave around them might well have been a palace, and her hood a crown. "Although I have no home, I have my daughter back. For that, I thank you all."

"But how did you find her? We've been looking for weeks," Zendric asked.

"We followed the riddle on the statues. I think Ssethedra put it there to lead us to her." Kellach replied, and the others nodded.

"Riddle?" Ssarine asked haughtily. "What riddle?"

"The statue Pralthamus presented to the city had part of a riddle carved on it in your language. We found another part of the riddle on the statue in Arren's warehouse, and we found the rest on Driskoll . . . " Kellach glanced shyly up at Driskoll. "Locky helped us translate them. The riddle told us how to make a compass, a light that would lead us to Ssethedra."

"A light?" Zendric looked quizzical.

Moyra nodded. "A brass nail, water, a dandelion, and red quartzite."

The medusa gasped. "That was a game that my daughter and I played back home! She would hide, and I would make a compass to come and find her. I had forgotten all about it." Ssarine knelt beside her daughter and drew the girl into her arms again. "My clever, clever girl."

"The bad man told me he had killed you, Mommy." The girl buried her head against her mother's velvet robe. "I didn't know what to do. I spelled it out, and just hoped. There had to be someone in the city who would help me! And my journal—I copied what he was saying into it and left it behind. I thought that if anyone found it, maybe they would figure out what he was doing and stop him."

"What a risk!" Ssarine said. "What if Arren had discovered what you were doing? The journal with his potions in it, the carvings on the statues . . . "

"What else could I do?" Ssethedra sniffled, throwing her

arms around her mother's neck. "I didn't think he could read our language. But I made it a riddle just in case he could. I kept running out of room on the statues to write, though."

"Brilliant!" Zendric ran his fingers through his hair, an amused and impressed grin spreading across his face. "We never even thought to look at the statues."

"I tried to give a note to one of the watchers at the prison, but Arren found out. He made me look at her. She was such a nice lady. I didn't want to do it!"

"Elisa," Kellach muttered.

"And there was a young watcher. He saw us sneaking out of the prison through the tunnel, but Arren caught him before he could report it to anyone. I had to look at him, too." Ssethedra looked at Driskoll and tears filled her eyes. "And then there was you."

"There, there, my darling," Ssarine's voice was soft and soothing.

Lochinvar chirped, sitting upright on Kellach's arm. The young meausa's tears seemed to have softened the clockwork dragon's feelings for the girl. His amethyst eyes whirled in sympathy.

"Useless creature," Ssarine whispered, a long, drawn-out hiss of breath following her words. "That dragon caused me no end of trouble, Zendric, I'll have you know. I'm well rid of it."

Despite her obvious relief, she straightened to an aristocratic height, keeping one arm tightly wrapped around her daughter.

"I thank you again, Ssarine," Zendric said, a spark of amusement in his eyes as he met Kellach's gaze. "Though it did not turn out as I had intended."

"Is . . . is he yours, then, Zendric?" Kellach's heart fell.

"He was. But, you see, we thought the dragon had been stolen," Zendric continued. "So, Ssarine used her magic to call him back."

Chuckling at the wide-eyed expression on their three faces, Zendric sagely hummed. "Oh, yes, you'd be surprised what this little fellow can do. Rather amazing."

He paused, then shook himself out of it, and smiled again. "In any case, we questioned the little fellow and discovered he'd been with you. But Ssarine couldn't get much out of all that chirping and whirring. So we let him go. When he realized you were planning to go down into Arren's cave, he came back to us and brought us here. That's a wise little dragon."

Moyra nodded, taking Lochinvar's head in her hands. "Lochinvar, I'm sorry. I shouldn't have said the things that I said about you." She stared into the violet eyes with a genuine regret, taking a deep breath before she continued, "I apologize."

The little dragon chirruped consolingly, rubbing his head against her cheek. "Moy-ree. Friends."

"Thanks." Moyra smiled, sheepishly.

"We rushed here to find you. But it looks like you didn't need much help." Zendric glanced down at Arren's limp body and laughed.

"Yeah," Kellach agreed, his hands upon his hips. "We had him completely at our mercy."

Moyra looked skeptical for a moment, then took her cue from Kellach and nodded.

"I'm impressed," said Zendric seriously. "Not many people could have gone up against Arren, much less his followers, and won. You have once again earned the names of Knights of the Silver Dragon, all three of you."

"Touching, I'm sure, but we have little time." Ssarine snapped her fingers in a quick rhythm.

Lochinvar suddenly froze. His wings furled, and his claws went limp. In an instant, he curled up, reverting to the strange puzzle ball. There was a sharp click.

The ball rolled off Kellach's shoulder and onto the floor, stopping near Ssarine's feet.

"This beast is useless now, Zendric." Ssarine gestured toward the little ball. She picked it up and held it to the torchlight appraisingly. "Once a clockwork animal is tuned to a particular wizard, it cannot be undone. I am sorry that I took such poor care of your reward. I shall melt it down and reforge it for you."

Kellach's jaw dropped, and even Moyra looked sad.

Driskoll piped up, "Oh, don't do that. We couldn't have gotten this far without Lochinvar."

"He's our friend!" Moyra said quickly, then looked down and bit her lip at the outburst. Even Driskoll looked surprised, and Moyra elbowed him in the ribs.

"No, that's not necessary, Ssarine," Zendric smiled. He tapped his finger against his chin thoughtfully.

Ssarine whispered, "You are certain? But . . . it will be of no use to you, Zendric. "

"Well . . . yes." With a sheepish smile, Zendric took the silver orb from the medusa's outstretched hand. "You see, the dragon was . . . well, it was intended to be a gift."

Zendric placed the egg into Kellach's hand. "Happy Promise Day, Kellach. I'm proud of you."

174

Kellach looked down at the orb in his hand and beamed.

"Now, we must be going. Come, my friends," Zendric began, turning toward the passageway. Before he could say anything else, a sudden noise in the corner caught their attention.

Arren groaned in pain, struggling to his knees. Zendric raised his hands to begin a spell, but before he could begin, the alchemist flashed out a vial from his sleeve.

"Don't try it, Zendric," the alchemist sneered. "This is poisonous gas. If I drop this, it will kill every breathing creature in this chamber within seconds. Myself included." Arren staggered to his feet, his threat clearly taking Zendric aback. "Oh, yes, I'm more than willing to give my life."

"Arren, no." Zendric's face turned sober, his hands gently lowering.

The alchemist began to back toward the far exit, his hand shaking around the greenish vial. "Let me go, Zendric. It's no use fighting."

But Arren did not notice Ssarine's hand slowly reaching for her hood. He turned toward the entrance and was met by a cold, yellow stare. Kellach saw flashes of snakes coiling up around the medusa's face, her face shielded from him by the rush of serpents that stretched out to capture Arren's shoulders in their poisonous fangs. Before the alchemist could drop the vial, his eyes were captured by hers.

"You may be immune to my daughter's gaze," Ssarine hissed, "but you are not immune to *mine*."

Kellach would never forget the horrified look on Arren's face, nor the shriek that came from his parted lips. Ssarine was older and a more experienced medusa than her daughter, and the stone took hold far more quickly. Arren's body stiffened, his hands clenched around the toxic vial. As Ssarine's serpents encased his head and shoulders like long hair, wrapping tightly around him and holding him still while the change took place.

When she stepped away at last, drawing the hood up over her features, Arren was nothing more than a marble statue, half kneeling as though in prayer, the vial hidden between his clasped hands.

CHAPTER

24

Fireworks exploded, their sparks igniting the evening sky.

Kellach, Moyra, and Driskoll sat against the obelisk in the center of Main Square, watching each explosion with *oohs* and *aahs*. All around them, the people of Curston celebrated the last evening of the Promise Festival with no idea of how close they had come to disaster.

"I'm glad Zendric managed to make enough antidote for everyone." Driskoll sighed, his eyes sleepy. He propped his head on his knees, staring out at Main Square. "It may take a few more days for them to shake off the drowsiness, but everyone should be fine."

"What about Elisa and the other watcher?" Moyra asked, her eyes alight with the fire in the sky.

"Dad said that Ssarine turned them back, the same way she did with Driskoll."

Kellach petted the little dragon on his shoulder, his fingers stroking the silvery scales. At his side, Driskoll grinned.

"There's Elisa now!" Driskoll pointed toward the edge of

Main Square. They could see a blonde woman laughing heartily among a group of watchers. Beside her, a young watcher was performing card tricks. "They're both just fine."

"Gult and all the other watchers are back on duty too. Pralthamus pardoned them for their crimes. It wasn't their fault after all. And Arren's looking dapper tonight, don't you think?" Kellach gestured grandly toward the statue near the center of the square. The light from the fireworks glinted off Arren's marble form.

The three kids laughed.

"I'm just glad Dad's back to normal again," Driskoll said. "How's Breddo?"

"He's still sleeping." Moyra said. Another firework lit the sky, the red and blue reflecting against her face. "Zendric said he got the heaviest dose of everyone. He'll probably be sick for a few more days. Zendric's going to come by and check him again tomorrow just to be sure."

"Just think, Breddo must have been in a cell just down the hall from Ssethedra. He might have even seen her going in and out or seen Elisa being brought in by Arren to be turned to stone." Driskoll shuddered. "What a nightmare."

Kellach turned to his brother. "Are you going to make a story about all this?"

Grinning, Driskoll nodded. "Yeah, I'd like to."

"Well," Kellach turned away, staring up at the sky. "Don't forget to include Driskoll, the Brave. Without him, we would never have solved the mystery." He saw the gleam in his brother's eyes. Driskoll sat up a little straighter, and both boys grinned.

"Do you think we'll ever see Ssarine or Ssethedra again?" Moyra asked. She didn't turn to look at the boys, keeping her eyes on the sky.

Kellach shook his head. "They won't stay where humans live. It's too dangerous for them. I expect they'll move on as soon as possible. If they're lucky, maybe they'll be able to go home again someday, to Medusa Island, and tell them all the good things about other races."

Kellach gazed up into the sky as the last of the fireworks fizzled, and the trio sat, lost for the moment in their thoughts.

Driskoll broke the silence. "I'm hungry. Let's go get something to eat." He stood up.

"You're always hungry, Driskoll." Moyra punched him playfully.

Driskoll shrugged. "I can't help it. I'm a growing boy. But don't worry." He grinned. "I'm not going to eat *any* cinnamon buns."

Kellach and Moyra laughed. They stood up and grabbed Driskoll's hands. Together, the three kids raced toward the market and were swallowed up by the shifting crowd.

SSETHEDRA'S RIDDLE

I send a plea that you might seek
a serpent's secret nest.
Where north is north
The needle spins
And east becomes the west.
To make a path that you can see,
At this you must not fail
A dish of water, red quartzite,
And one brass nail.
Place a sun upon the stone,
and you will swiftly see
The secret of the stone is this:
the light will follow me.

A young thief.
A wizard's apprentice.
A twelve-year-old boy.
Meet the Knights of
the Silver Dragon!

SECRET OF THE SPIRITKEEPER
Matt Forbeck

Can Moyra, Kellach, and Driskoll unlock the secret of the
spiritkeeper in time to rescue their beloved wizard friend?

August 2004

RIDDLE IN STONE
Ree Soesbee

Will the Knights unravel the statue's riddle
before more people turn to stone?

August 2004

SIGN OF THE SHAPESHIFTER
Dale Donovan and Linda Johns

Can Kellach and Driskoll find the shapeshifter
before he ruins their father?

October 2004

EYE OF FORTUNE
Denise R. Graham

Does the fortuneteller's prophecy spell doom
for the Knights? Or unheard-of treasure?

December 2004

For ages 8 and up

THE NEW ADVENTURES

JOIN A GROUP OF FRIENDS AS THEY UNLOCK MYSTERIES OF THE DRAGONLANCE® WORLD!

TEMPLE OF THE DRAGONSLAYER
Tim Waggoner

Nearra has lost all memory of who she is. With newfound friends, she ventures to an ancient temple where she may uncover her past. Visions of magic haunt her thoughts. And someone is watching.

July 2004

THE DYING KINGDOM
Stephen D. Sullivan

In a near-forgotten kingdom, an ancient evil lurks. As Nearra's dark visions grow stronger, her friends must fight for their lives.

July 2004

THE DRAGON WELL
Dan Willis

Battling a group of bandits, the heroes unleash the mystic power of a dragon well. And none of them will ever be the same.

September 2004

RETURN OF THE SORCERESS
Tim Waggoner

When Nearra and her friends confront the wizard who stole her memory, their faith in each other is put to the ultimate test.

November 2004

For ages 10 and up

JOIN THE

AND RECEIVE A COLLECTIBLE
SILVER DRAGON MINIATURE!

YOUR SILVER DRAGON MINIATURE IS FREE!

Follow these steps to become a **Knights of the Silver Dragon** member.
Important: If you are under 13, one of your parents will need to sign this
form. If your parent does not sign this form, we won't be able to enroll
you in KNIGHTS OF THE SILVER DRAGON.

1) Read this.
By filling out this form you are enrolling in **Knights of the Silver Dragon**.
This will make you eligible to receive:

• A silver dragon miniature and other collectibles;
• Information about upcoming books;
• And other cool information about the **Knights of the Silver Dragon!**

2) Please provide your contact information.

First Name: _____   Phone: _____

Last Name: _____   Email: _____

Address: _____   ☐ Male   ☐ Female

City: _____   Date of Birth (month/day/year):

State/Province: _____   _____

Zip/Postal Code: _____   Country* (check one): ☐ U.S.A. ☐ Canada

*Offer valid in the U.S. and Canada.

3) Get your parents to sign this form after reading the "Parents" information if you are under 13.

Parent/Guardian's Printed Name: _____

Parent/Guardian's Signature: _____

4) Send completed and signed membership/consent form to:

> **Knights of the Silver Dragon**
> C/O KP Fulfillment House
> 20014 70th Avenue South
> Kent, WA 98032

Your Silver Dragon Miniature costs nothing!
Send your membership and consent form in now!

Limit one **Knights of the Silver Dragon** membership and dragon miniature collectible per person. Miniature offer valid while supplies last. Allow 6 to 8 weeks for delivery.

PARENTS:

Your child would like to register for Knights of the Silver Dragon membership from Wizards of the Coast. When you send in this form, your child will be sent membership materials including a dragon miniature collectible (while supplies last), information about upcoming books published by Mirrorstone Books, and other printed materials related to Knights of the Silver Dragon, Mirrorstone, and Wizards of the Coast. From time to time, your child may also be sent other physical mailings and emails. In the future, membership in Knights of the Silver Dragon may also include access to a special area of the Wizards of the Coast web site, where your child may be able to change his contact information and participate in online surveys. Before we can allow your child's personal and demographic information to be viewed and modified online, we want to notify you about our online information collection practices and obtain your permission. We ask that you first read through the "Note to Parents" in the Wizards Website Privacy Statement (http://www.wizards.com/parents), which identifies the personal information that Wizards of the Coast collects from children online and the way we handle such information. If you cannot connect to our web site, our customer service team can provide you with the information and answer any other questions (800-424-6496).

When you have finished reading the parental information materials referenced above, please sign this registration form where it says "Parent/Guardian's Signature."

Please note that once you have signed and sent us this form, you always have the ability to: (i.) review your child's personal information collected online; (ii.) request that we delete your child's personal information online; (iii.) stop us from further using or collecting additional personal information online about your child without gaining new permission from you. To do so, please contact us using the information provided above.